# BURGUNDY

## IN THE

# BLUEGRASS

### WINE TALES FROM KENTUCKY

## CRAIG CAUDILL

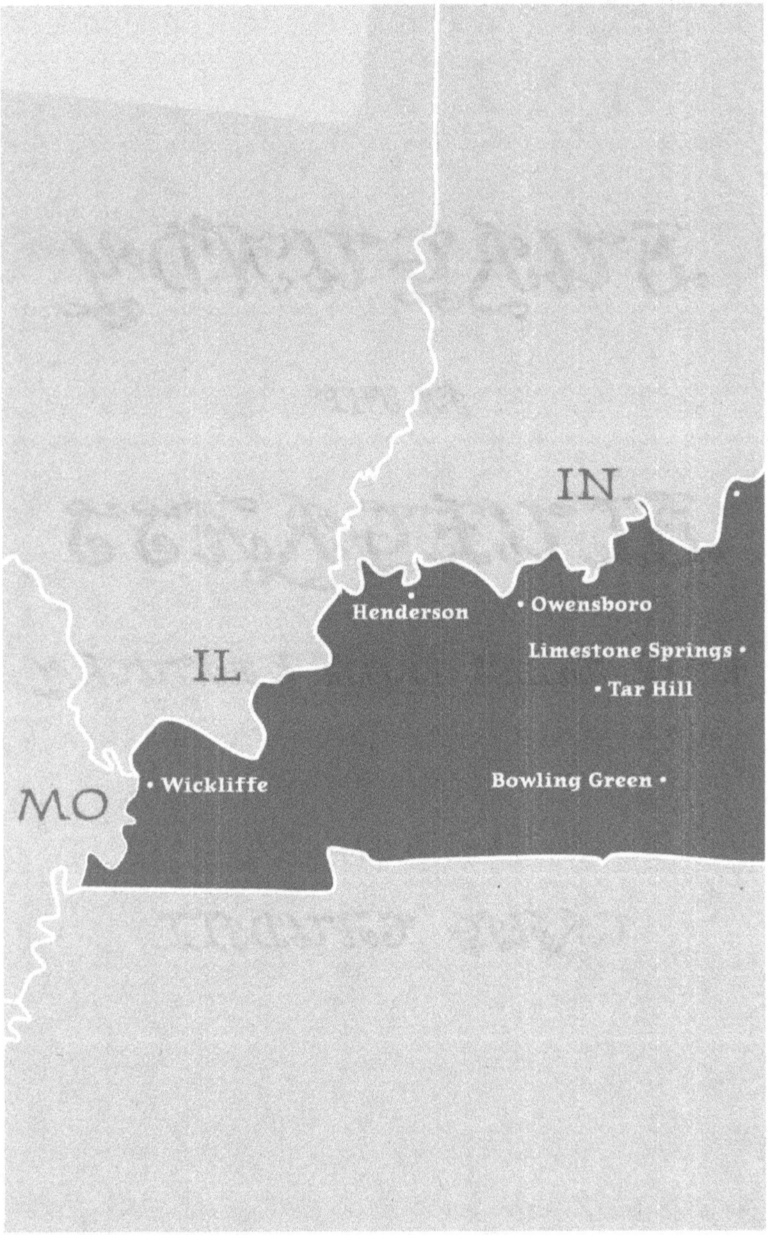

IN
Henderson
Owensboro
Limestone Springs
Tar Hill
IL
Wickliffe
Bowling Green
MO

OH

Florence

• Napoleon
Warsaw •

Louisville

• Paris

WV

Waddy •        • Lexington        • Wrigley
   Versailles •   • Wilmore     • Frenchburg
Lawrenceburg •      • Richmond
            • Harrodsburg
      Danville •              • Booneville
Monticello •    • Somerset      • Hazard

VA

      • Boone's Ridge

TN

NC

For my wife, Jo, and our family.

# CONTENTS

# CONTENTS

# AMOS BREND AND THE FORT JEFF BLUES

Scads of cheesemongers, packed like sardines in the stuffy hotel banquet room, broke into oohs and aahs when the punctilious head judge at the dais finally announced this year's champion. Amos Brend swiveled in his seat, searching for Eileen de Boer to see the expression on her face. She had already gotten up and was marching toward the exit. He stepped quickly through the side door near the mezzanine entrance to catch up to her. "Wait!" he called out. She turned to face him. "I'm so sorry," Amos said in a concerned tone. She looked down and said nothing. "I know you thought this would be your year, Eileen."

"Got beat by a flavored goat cheese. Hell, anybody can make that crap," she declared.

"When will you be returning home?"

All the fight had gone out of her now. "I'm leaving in the morning. It's about an eight-hour trip."

"Could I escort you to dinner this evening? I've got a reservation at seven."

"Thanks, Amos. I think I'll take you up on that. Fetch me out front of the Hilton at ten till."

Amos Brend had been managing director of the Amerique Fromage Championnat, otherwise known as the American Cheese

Championship, for thirteen years. He had gotten to know Eileen de Boer, believing that one day they would name her cheese the best in the United States. She had come close lots of times, like this year, but had never quite gotten over the hump. He felt bad for her because, being a cheese connoisseur himself, he found her Fort Jeff Blue to be the best thing he had ever tasted.

Eileen, in her late forties, wasn't a thin-boned classic beauty, but she was damned good-looking. You could tell that she worked with her hands by the calluses. Her careful grooming made that feature not so obvious, unless she was sipping a goblet of vino across the table from a man in a dimly lit Italian eatery as she was at that moment. "What kind of wine is this? It's superb."

Amos grabbed the bottle, leaned to the light, and said, "Aquitonia cabernet. Aquitonia Winery in Limestone Springs, Kentucky. Hey, wait a minute, that's where the champion cheesemaker hails from this year. What a coincidence."

"I've never heard of the winner's shop before."

"This is the first year they've entered. Ibex Aisne. The woman who represents them told me the name was from an ibex, which is an Alpine goat, and Aisne, the region in France where her family had a goat farm."

"Did you taste her stuff?"

"I certainly did," Amos replied. "Goat cheese with honey and fennel fronds wrapped in smoked grape leaves soaked in bourbon. Rather gimmicky I thought, but it had a good flavor. Not in the same class as your magnificent blue. The presentation was kind of interesting. The log was split down the middle and butterflied. Honestly, I think the fragrant grape leaves carried the day."

Eileen ordered linguini and clams with red sauce. Amos always got the special. She asked, "So, will you make your customary trip to the winning cheese operation to get pictures for the newsletter?"

"In two weeks. It seems that Limestone Springs, Kentucky, is along the rail line from Bardstown to Louisville. Myra Lerastelle, the proprietor, suggested I take the lunch train over to her place."

"What's the deal with that?"

"Oh, it's a tourist trap, I suppose. You board the train in Bardstown, they ply you with food and bourbon, and then stop in Limestone Springs so people can get out and shop for thirty minutes or so."

Eileen reflected, "I bet she sells a lot of chevre that way. My place is in the middle of nowhere."

"Why don't you meet me in Bardstown and tag along. We can have a little fun."

"When is that?" She brought up the calendar on her phone, waiting for him to say the date. After some playful banter on the way back to the Hilton, she agreed to join him.

Eileen's Mississippi River Creamery was on the banks of the Mississippi south of Wickliffe, Kentucky, just north of Fort Jefferson Hill Park on US Highway 62. She built the place after her husband, Vincent, drowned in the Missouri River on a fishing trip twelve years ago. The two of them owned a bistro in St. Louis at the time that specialized in interesting wines and cheeses. She sold the restaurant, and it took her a year to perfect the blue cheese that she began entering in competitions.

Fort Jeff Blue was an English-style blue cheese produced from firm, tangy curd run through a mill to yield small, irregular-shaped curds, tossed with salt and placed in a cylindrical mold. A gang of very thin needles mounted on a fixture was pressed in the wheel to get air to the mold for propagating the spores. The finished product was ready in six months. In the hierarchy of categories, blue-veined cheeses were considered far superior to goat cheeses, but somehow, it didn't work like that this year.

Sunlight washed the inside of the Third Street train depot in Bardstown that was now loaded with lunch passengers. Amos Brend sat in a green fiberglass seat reading a newspaper, awaiting the arrival of Eileen de Boer. She rushed through the door and looked around the room to find him. "How's my favorite turophile?" she asked brightly.

"Good. And my favorite casei culturer?" He dropped the paper and stood to hug her.

The dining cars had enormous windows, wood paneling, gray tablecloths, and red accordion napkins tucked in blue water glasses. Amos and Eileen both had the Kentucky Hot Brown followed by a snort of neat bourbon. The train steamed through the countryside and skirted a beautiful forest of virgin timber that intermittently shadowed the tracks. The loud engine slowed as the destination came into view.

Limestone Springs, east of Interstate 65, west of Jim Beam Distillery, was a hopping place years back. It had a working train depot, post office, and its share of whiskey operations. Nowadays, it boasted a dinky winery and obscure cheesemaker, soon to be world famous. Amos shielded his eyes from the sun and searched for the Ibex Aisne sign. When he located it, he could see Myra Lerastelle standing in the doorway waving at him. Amos grabbed Eileen's elbow and guided her in Myra's direction. Formal introductions were made and the three of them moved into the retail area to look at the refrigerator of cheeses. Some packages were Valençay style, and the small logs of goat cheese were covered in ash, smoked paprika, orange annatto, or various kinds of leaves.

Eileen said, "Congratulations on winning the championship."

Myra smiled and said, "Thank you." She was a small woman with a pleasant, oval face and blue eyes that matched her apron. Her auburn hair, covered with a hairnet, had been done in a thick pageboy, shorter in the back than the front.

"Are you from Kentucky?" Amos asked.

"Heavens no. I'm an Oregonian hippie. My husband left me, so I decided to start a new life here. We were making chevre from buttermilk since we didn't have any cultures. One day I put some cheese balls in the smoker, and they came out really tasty. That's how I got onto smoking the grape leaves, which, of course, are now on the cheese that won the award."

"Soaking them in bourbon doesn't hurt either," Amos added.

"Good for you," Eileen said. "Where are you getting the grape leaves?"

"Oh, the guy that owns that winery sells them to me." She looked through the window at the building next door that had the name Aquitonia in teal script letters mounted on the front. "He's helped me with a lot of things."

"We've tasted, well, finished off a bottle of his cabernet. It's exceptional. Look, I'm going to run over there while you all take some pictures. Hopefully, I can pick up a few bottles of that cab," Eileen said.

Durbin "Ben" Jannuzzo rolled into Limestone Springs some years ago to open an artisan winery. What brought him there were the scraggly cabernet grapevines once tended to by a reclusive man who had died, leaving an heir to dispose of the property. Ben bought the vineyard, whipped life back into it, and erected a little chateau to make and sell wine. Shortly thereafter, Myra put in the cheese operation, and the two of them began enjoying each other's company.

Eileen tramped through the front door of Aquitonia Winery and was instantly blocked by a throng of people trying to pay for wine before the train began the trip back. The two men at the tasting bar and cash register seemed overwhelmed. A third man appeared from the back. Eileen didn't look at him closely at first. She did a double take when he peered in her direction. Suddenly, she fainted, falling in a heap. The people who saw her go down shouted for help. Ben Jannuzzo made his way over to her and knelt, waiting for her to come to. When she did, she muttered, "Vincent, is that you?"

"Are you okay, ma'am?"

Eileen sat up, and Ben helped her to her feet. "Yes, I guess it's stuffy in here. When I saw you, I thought you were my husband, who drowned twelve years ago."

"Well, my name is Ben Jannuzzo. Can I get you a drink of water?"

"No. I came in here to buy some of your cabernet." She straightened her hair and wiped it off her face.

"How many bottles would you like?" Ben asked obsequiously.

"Three would be great."

He placed them in a carton for her to show the cashier. "By the way, what was your husband's name?" he asked.

"Vincent de Boer."

When Eileen walked out of the winery, Amos was standing off to the side. He asked, "What was all the commotion about?"

"It was really close quarters in there. I fainted. I'm okay now," she remarked, hoping he would leave it at that. "I'll tell you more on the train ride back." Eileen handed him the trio of cabernet bottles to carry.

The dining car swayed gently as the locomotive reached speed on the return trip to Bardstown. The lunch crowd had loosened up considerably, and the conversation, with guffaws sprinkled in, got louder. "Are you sure you're okay?" Amos probed.

"Yes. The man who owns that winery back there, I think he said his name was Ben Jannuzzo, is my husband, Vincent. I thought he drowned, but he must have faked his death somehow."

Amos sat up in his seat and blurted, "How can that be?"

"I don't know, but I'm going to find out. That Myra woman, I've seen her before. She came into our bistro several years ago, just before Vincent drowned. She's got something to do with this. I'll bet they came up with a scheme to run off together."

"Eileen, that's incredible. Are you sure it's Vincent?"

"I was married to the man for ten years. I know his face like the back of my hand. It's him."

"So, what are you going to do?"

"I don't know yet," she replied.

Amos gazed out the window with a glassy expression. He turned back to her and said, "There's one way to clear it up. Hire a private detective to do a background check on him."

"That's a good idea," she affirmed. "Shall we have another shot of bourbon before we get in?"

Amos smiled as he waved the server over.

Eileen hugged Amos before she got in her car to leave. "When can you come and visit me at my place on the river?" she asked.

He said, "You name the time, I'll be there. Let me know what you find out about your husband." After he pulled away to the north in his car, Eileen headed west in hers. In a half hour, she was back in Limestone Springs, standing in Ibex Aisne, talking to Myra Lerastelle.

"I wanted to come back through on the way home since I didn't get a chance to buy your award-winning cheese."

Myra opened the refrigerator to retrieve a package of Drunken Honfen and handed it to her. "It's on the house."

"Only if you'll let me send you some of my Fort Jeff Blue."

"Deal."

"You know, my husband and I used to have a bistro in St. Louis, and I remember you coming in our place once. Oh, gosh, it must be at least twelve years ago now." Eileen focused on Myra's expression to see how she would take that shot across the bow.

"Twelve years ago, I was in Oregon, still married to my husband." She walked back behind the retail counter and leaned forward on straight arms. "Do you still have the restaurant?"

Eileen stared back at Myra in distrust. "No. My husband drowned while on a fishing trip. I sold it and started making cheese in Western Kentucky, on the Mississippi River."

"I'm sorry to hear that." A honk from a car blared through the front wall. "Oh, that's probably Ben from next door. We're going to Louisville to do some grocery shopping. It was nice meeting you."

"You too," Eileen replied. She looked through the window and saw Ben Jannuzzo staring at her.

Eileen de Boer pulled into her place that evening at suppertime, exhausted from driving on the roads that had to be traversed when traveling west across the middle of the state. She had mulled over the circumstances of Vincent's death the whole ride home, and no explanation for his reappearance seemed plausible.

Her cottage on the banks of the river, down from the cheese factory, was all glass on the back. The dazzling sun ricocheted off the south-flowing, muddy Mississippi, casting an orange glare on the furniture in the sitting room. She put a frozen pesto pizza in the oven, opened a bottle of Aquitonia and a package of Drunken Honfen before flopping on the davenport. The wine and goat cheese tasted good together. She grabbed her phone in jealousy and began Googling private detectives.

~ ~ ~

On the way back from Louisville, Myra said, "Eileen de Boer worries me. She's unpredictable."

Ben said, "She's harmless. Don't worry about her."

"She's been trying to win best in show for years, and some flashy new cheese like ours aces her out every time."

"She told me I looked like her dead husband," Ben said.

"That's not good," Myra concluded.

~ ~ ~

Fort Jeff Blue sales were picking up again seasonally based on another high finish in the national championship. Eileen kept busy filling orders and making more. One afternoon a FedEx package came marked confidential. She tore it open to find background data on Ben. She went into her office and began poring over the report. After scribbling a handwritten note, Eileen jumped up and opened the cooler to grab a package of her blockbuster blue cheese to send to Ibex Aisne as she promised Myra she would do. The note she inserted said:

> *Myra,*
>
> *Your cheese is absolutely wonderful! I hope you enjoy mine as much as I did yours.*
>
> *I'm not sure if you know this, but Ben Jannuzzo isn't who he says he is. Be careful.*
>
> *Eileen de Boer*

Ben appeared in the doorway of Myra's shop. "What did you need to see me about?"

"I told you that de Boer woman was unpredictable. Look at this." She waved the note at him. He scooted over to retrieve it. While he was reading what it said, Myra sarcastically asked him, "Just exactly who are you?"

Ben looked up at her and chuckled. "Yeah, right."

~ ~ ~

Amos Brend heard his phone ring. "Nice to hear from you, Eileen. Are you doing well?"

"Yes. I just got the report on Ben Jannuzzo. There is no record of him before ten years ago."

Amos switched the phone to his other hand and replied, "I did a little checking too. Myra said that her husband had left her, which caught my interest. I had a man in Oregon find a picture of him. It's Ben Jannuzzo."

"I don't believe it," Eileen retorted.

"Well, I guess they figured not being married in Kentucky would be good for business."

"Come on, Amos, you don't really believe that, do you? He's my husband, and he'll be coming for me."

"That's ridiculous. He's interested in Myra Lerastelle."

Late the next afternoon, Eileen heard a knock on the side door of her cottage. She released the deadbolt and said, "Come on in, I've been expecting you," as she walked over to the wall facing the river.

"Really? We didn't talk about me visiting you today."

"So, Vincent, just exactly how did you come back to life?" Eileen asked.

"What are you talking about?"

"I poisoned you and threw your body in the Missouri River. I went to a lot of trouble making it look like a fishing accident." She turned away from the windows to look at him.

"Why did you do that?"

"Because you made fun of me when I told you that I was going to make the best blue cheese in the world." She seemed demon possessed now. "Well, I guess you get the last laugh after all. That little girl you've taken up with beat me out."

"Eileen, I'm Amos Brend, not Vincent, or Ben. Do you recognize me?" She staggered forward, fell into his arms, and began sobbing. "You're going to be all right," he said to soothe her.

~ ~ ~

The following year, the head judge at the American Cheese Championship stood to announce that Fort Jeff Blue had been selected best in the land. Amos Brend rose and stated, "Ladies and gentlemen, the owner of Mississippi River Creamery couldn't make it this year. I'll make sure she receives this award. Thank you." The applause was somewhat anemic since the person who had worked so hard to win the prize wasn't there.

At that moment, the captain of the tugboat maneuvering the coal barge down the Mississippi picked up his pouch of Red Man chewing tobacco, grabbed a wad, and stuck it in his mouth. He spit out the stems and wiped his lips out of habit. A pair of high-powered binoculars were lying on the deck by the window. The captain put them to his face as he did customarily to peek in the houses along the shoreline, hoping to see something interesting for once. What he saw that time through the all-glass wall of the cottage he had passed many times was a woman stabbing a man in the back.

Amos Brend had told Eileen de Boer to expect him two weeks after the championship. She let him in the side door when he arrived, and then said, "Come in, come in, wonderful to see you."

He gave her a long hug and kiss on the cheek. "You finally did it! Congratulations."

"Thank you. It feels good to win. Can I get you a cup of coffee?" she asked.

"That would be great," he replied. Eileen left the sitting room for the kitchen. "By the way, have you heard?"

"Heard what?"

"Ben Jannuzzo has been missing for two weeks. Just disappeared."

"No, I hadn't heard." She returned and handed him a coffee cup and saucer.

"Eileen, have you ever considered getting married again? You know, a husband doesn't have to testify against his wife in a court of law." Amos gave her a salute with his coffee cup and smile.

# THE HAZARD OF TAILOR-MADE CRYPTOCURRENCY

Brock Skinner's $280,000 Lamborghini swept into Hazard from the south, on US 15, right before noon, causing every head to turn that heard the growl of the powerful V10 engine. Part of what profligate showboats paid for when they purchased the penultimate driving machine was that fantastic sound. Noisy. Fierce. Not to be messed with. Brock cruised into a frowzy gas station to use the restroom, and when he returned to his car, two rough-looking customers were standing there. The roly-poly gent in bib overalls piped up, "We don't see too many cars like this around here."

"Really?" Brock was even less likely to be messed with than his car. The cords of his neck were taut, and the back of his head was flat and tall. He had muscular, square shoulders, and ears pinned against his head. "Imagine that."

The other fellow, a simian knuckle dragger, asked rhetorically, "You making fun of us, boy?"

Brock got back in the Lamborghini and rolled down the window. "Yes, as a matter of fact, I am," he answered decisively. Mister Ape moved around to face Skinner at the car door. He could see the nine-millimeter handgun lying in the passenger seat. "Was there something else I can help you with?"

"I'm good, for the moment," Mister Ape whispered in a guttural voice.

"Say, maybe you can help me." Brock intended to defuse the situation. "Would you happen to know where Vigneron Winery is?"

"Why, sure. You go back the way you came for, oh, say, five or six hundred miles, and it's on the right," Mister Bib chimed in.

"Well, thank you." He started the car and revved the engine, waiting for Mister Bib to get out of the way. When he didn't, Brock backed out of the gas station and wheeled up onto the highway heading through town.

Vigneron Winery, north of Hazard, was the lone vineyard in Southeast Kentucky. Skinner saw the sign for it and followed the road leading there. The winery had been scabbed onto the side of a hill, but the serpentine rows of grapevines had been planted on the gently sloping section of the property. It was the prettiest wine operation he had ever seen. The building had nine gables and rough-hewn, knotty pine siding with vertical battens at the joints. The veranda was packed with green tables and chairs, affording as many guests as possible the opportunity to take in the million-dollar view over the long valley and edge of the ravine. Brock eased into a parking space away from other cars and walked through the entrance door looking for the owner.

"Maude, how long has it been?"

"Oh, Brock, how nice to see you again." Maude Sutherland was thirty-one years old, three years younger than her one brother, Marcel. She stood 5' 10" and neared 160 pounds, but of course, no one knew that for sure. Maude was all curves and had the face of an angel. Marcel lent her a million dollars to construct the winery seven years ago. It was now producing and had become a weekend destination for vacationers around Kentucky and the four surrounding states.

"Man, this place is beautiful. What a fantastic job you've done with it." He hugged her and held her hands for a few seconds.

"Thanks. I love it here." She hooked his arm and said, "Let's go into my office."

Every inch of Maude's walls in her office was covered with framed photography, a pictorial history of the winery. Her desk was piled with paper detritus, not yet filed or thrown out. "Business doing well?" he asked. They sat together on a comfy leather couch facing the desk.

"It was just starting to, and then I got this." She handed him the letter.

"I take it this is why Marcel asked me to come." He looked at her, and then the note.

> *Maude Sutherland,*
>
> *We have information that someone is interested in poisoning your grapevines. We are not sure why they would want to do that, but if you would like us to prevent that from happening, for a fee, we can protect your vineyard. You can pay us $20,000 on the first day of each month, through the Bitcoin mixer: Fat Wallet. Address funds to 8aYN43rt91.*
>
> *Veraison Security*

Brock said, "High-tech criminal using a low-tech shakedown."

"What should I do?"

"Is there any way to get to the grapevines from the back or sides of the property?" he asked.

"The ravine protects one side and the hilltop the other. I don't know about the back."

"There are three options I can think of. First, pay it. Second, get some security in here. Third, try to catch them in the act. In any case, I want to see if I can find out who's doing this."

Maude raised her eyebrows and arms, saying, "How?"

"The person must figure your brother will pay it. How many people know that Marcel is backing you?"

"Nobody. He absolutely forbade me from telling anyone," she replied defiantly. "Well, he told you, I guess."

"It's reasonable to assume that he would be there if you needed money for something like this. He could have told somebody himself, I suppose. Maybe a customer," Brock suggested.

"He's got thousands of those."

Marcel Sutherland and Brock Skinner became friends while they were attending the University of Kentucky. Marcel told Brock of the scheme he had cooked up, and that he needed investors. Brock liked the thought, so he took a quarter of a million dollars he had inherited and invested all of it in Marcel's deal, and what a deal it was. They were both multimillionaires now, thanks to Marcel's great execution of the marvelous idea he had.

Sutherland Tailoring opened digital body measuring booths in many states in America. The way it worked for people wanting quick delivery of custom-tailored clothing was to come to a booth, get digitally measured wearing only underwear, and then select the garments with the desired specifications for each piece such as fabric, style, and fit. The secret to the business was in the programming that converted body measurements into cloth patterns to be cut and sewn.

Marcel hired designers to broaden the product line, programmers to facilitate manufacturing of garments, and contract sewing operations to produce the clothing quickly on demand. He held onto the domestic business and franchised operations throughout the rest of the world. He and Brock couldn't spend the money they had made in ten lifetimes.

Skinner stood and said, "Come on, Maude, let's get a bite of lunch. Would you care to drive the Lamborghini?"

"Uh, no."

"One of these days, you must," he encouraged.

~ ~ ~

Marcel Sutherland's offices were in downtown Harrodsburg. He set up shop there because two old sewing operations were nearby that he did business with and eventually bought. They now served as test sites for sewing new garments and debugging software. Brock marched straight into Marcel's office without checking with anybody, and said, "I'm going to marry your sister."

"You're what?" Marcel got up from his desk chair, strolled over to shake Skinner's hand.

"She doesn't know it yet."

"You have my blessing if you can catch the snake trying to rip her off."

"So, let's talk about that." Brock walked over to the corner of the office, leaned on the wall, and put his hands in his pockets. "We're not going to find 'em tracing the cryptocurrency. We need a lucky break."

"How do we get one?" Marcel sat back down behind his desk.

"I figure among your customers, there's a crook in tailored clothing who visited the winery, and putting you and your sister together, saw an opportunity to blackmail her, hence you."

"You're talking needle in a haystack. I pledge to keep customer information confidential."

"Not if criminal activity is involved," Brock rebutted.

Marcel opened a laptop on his desk, typed on it, and carried it over to the birch worktable near where Brock was standing. "There you go. See if you can find a needle."

Brock sifted through customer data files for hours, sorting by name, address, and size. He said to Marcel, "Looks like some customers get measured more than once even though you have their size on file."

"Yes. They start fresh instead of looking up their account."

"Okay. So, here are two anomalies of people with the same measurements, under two different names. What are the chances of any two people being identical in size?"

Marcel stepped over to the worktable and looked over Brock's shoulder. "Zero."

"Ergo, these two people are going by different names."

"Who are they?"

Brock hovered over the first name. "Jalen Millhouse of Cleveland, Ohio, is also Karim Clanton of Hazard, Kentucky." He scrolled down to the second one. "And Margo Millhouse of Cleveland is Rosemarie Clanton."

Marcel said, "Bring up Google Earth. Put in that Hazard address." They drilled down to the close-up of the site. It was the property that backed up to Vigneron Winery. There was an oblong log cabin and detached garage on the small farm. "I'll be damned."

"Something's fishy. The people owning land close to the winery would be obvious suspects."

"Google Jalen and Margo Millhouse," Marcel said.

Brock read several articles about them, and finally said, "The boat of Jalen and Margo Millhouse was found capsized on Lake

Erie. The bodies were never recovered. Millhouse's company owed the banks millions of dollars. It was put into bankruptcy after the couple's disappearance."

Marcel concluded, "I think you've found the needle."

"Best I pay a visit to the Clantons." Skinner saluted Marcel as he departed.

~ ~ ~

Brock Skinner pulled into Vigneron Winery again the next morning and saw Maude bent over in the flower bed under the carved, eponymous granite sign. She straightened up and waved. The early day sunshine brightened her face and atmosphere around her. He put the pistol under his belt before meeting her next to the flowers. "Your brother says hi. I told him how beautiful I think you are. Now I'm telling you."

"All the men I meet tell me that." She kissed him on the lips. "But I only kiss a small percentage of them."

"Thank goodness. Otherwise, you'd be married now, off in obscurity somewhere."

"What's with the gun?" she asked.

"I'm going to the back of the property to look around."

The half-mile trek through the vines ended at a five-foot-high wire fence with metal posts every fifteen feet. One section by the ravine was loose and could be pulled back to drive through. He unhooked and re-hooked the wire to enter the property owned by the Clantons on foot. Brock worked his way alongside the ravine until he came to the rear of the detached garage. When he peeked around the corner at the log cabin, he saw Mister Bib and Mister Ape pop out the back door.

"Come on out, we see you," Mister Ape yelled. Skinner took a calculated risk and began running toward the vineyard. Two shotgun booms came next accompanied by a pinging ricochet. He got to the fence, went through, and sprinted between the vines until he emerged in the parking lot, short of breath.

Maude cried out, "What happened?"

"Your neighbors shot at me. I have a hunch they'll be coming for me."

"What are you going to do?"

"Wait for them." Brock sat on the veranda with his gun hidden and head on a swivel. Right after lunch, a couple pulled in, got out, and marched into the winery building.

Maude approached them and asked, "Can I help you, folks?"

"Yes, we own the farm at the back of your winery. Two of our hands chased a trespasser off. He escaped through here. They said he was a man who drives a fancy sports car. He was seen in town a couple of days ago."

Brock stood, stuck the gun down his lower back, and inserted himself in the conversation. "That would be me."

The man turned to face him and said, "I told my men to shoot to kill if they see you on our land again. I suggest you leave town before something bad happens to you."

"Is that a threat?"

"Take it however you want."

The woman interrupted, "Come on, Karim, let's get out of here."

"You're not Karim Clanton or Jalen Millhouse, and you're not Rosemarie or Margo. Who are you people?" Brock asked.

"We're the Clantons. Now, leave us alone," he retorted.

"The same goes for you. We're not paying you a cent. If anything happens to the grapevines on this property, I'm coming for you." Brock jabbed the man in the chest.

"I don't know what you're talking about," he spat while wiping away Skinner's hand. The couple tried to look mystified on the way back to their car. It didn't work.

Maude grabbed Skinner's arm. "How do you know those people aren't the Clantons?"

"Because I learned how to interpret the size code in the database of your brother's customers. Both of them are at least two inches shorter than the people we're looking for."

"So, what's going on here?"

Brock didn't answer. "Do you know the sheriff in Hazard?"

"Sure. He comes around every few days."

"Call him."

Sheriff Nathan Connors walked into Vigneron an hour later. "What's the problem, Maude?"

"This is a friend of mine, Brock Skinner. I'll let him tell you."

Brock offered his hand. "Sheriff. There's something peculiar going on at the farm over there." He pointed toward the back of the winery.

Connors turned his head and replied, "You mean at the Clanton place?"

"Yes. A couple claiming to be the Clantons just left here, and I'm sure they're somebody else. I would like for you to ride over with me and see if you can identify them."

"Funny you say that." The sheriff appeared to be puzzled. "The Clantons bought that place two years ago, and I can't say that I've ever seen them there. Ellis and Dob Brunnell keep it up. I think they live there."

"I call them Mister Ape and Mister Bib. I'm sure you know which is which," Brock added. "Look, why don't Maude and I follow you in my car. Let's go over there right now."

21

"Suits me." Sheriff Connors got in his cruiser and called headquarters to declare his mission. He left the parking lot, heading around the mountain to get to the other side. Both cars drove into the gravel driveway and parked off in the grass. After they got out, Sheriff Connors commented, "I don't think anybody's here." He leaned forward and began striding to the fortress of a house.

Suddenly, the door to the garage flew open. The engine of a monster truck gurgled to life. The driver, Mister Ape, hit the gas and came roaring toward Brock and Maude. They lunged to the other side of the driveway. The gigantic truck tire smashed into the Lamborghini, mangling the driver's side, leaving it flattened and broken up. The sheriff saw what happened, jumped in his cruiser, turned on the siren, and gave chase.

Skinner blurted, "I'm gonna get that son of a bitch." He looked at the Lamborghini in disgust. "Let's go in the house and see what we can find."

Everything personal had been cleared out. It appeared that a computer had once been on the desk in the main room, but was gone now. He pulled open the drawer to find paper for a printer and office supplies left behind. Something else was there, a computer memory stick.

Maude heard a vehicle pull in the driveway, so she went to the window. Connors had returned, apparently thrown off the truck's trail. When he came in, he said, "They went off road. I couldn't follow them."

"Sheriff, do you think you can get a search warrant for this place?" Brock asked.

"Sure. What are we looking for?"

"Jalen and Margo Millhouse. I think they were posing as Karim and Rosemarie Clanton. I have a hunch the Brunnell brothers

killed and buried them. They found another couple to imperson-
ate the Clantons for some reason, which I'm going to find out."

Brock called a wrecker to haul the broken-up car to a dealer in
Louisville. When they got back to the winery, he went to
Maude's computer to insert the memory stick. The larger of the
two files had a hundred extortion letters addressed to wineries
around the country. The amounts being demanded ranged from
$50 to $200 per month, most at $100. The bitcoin address for
payment was different than the one on the letter Maude received.
The other file only had her letter in it.

"Look at that," she said.

"Yeah. My guess is Jalen and Margo Millhouse faked their deaths
and became the Clantons. To make money, they came up with
an anonymous extortion scheme. The Brunnells found out about
it and thought they could do it better."

"So, why the imposters?"

"Two reasons I can think of. They needed a couple to appear as
the property owners, and they would have to be people who
knew how to set up a Fat Wallet account through bitcoin."

"So, all four of them are in on it. Upping the demand to twenty
thousand a month wasn't that smart a move. Surely they knew it
would cause an investigation."

"Those people are stupid and greedy. They must have figured
your brother had the money and would pay it," Brock surmised.

"How are we going to catch them?" Maude asked.

"We don't really have to. The deal is dead. I want to though because those jackasses destroyed my car." He studied the letter to
Maude for several minutes before calling Sutherland.

"This is Marcel."

"Brock. I remember the size codes in the database were fifteen alphanumeric characters. Do you use any codes that are ten digits long?"

Marcel hesitated for a moment. "Oh, yes we do. The item numbers on invoices are ten digits."

Skinner sat up straight and focused on the Fat Wallet account number on the letter to Maude. "See if you can find who bought this item." He read off the ten letters and numbers deliberately.

"Okay, I'll text it to you if I find it." Marcel cut the line. In an hour, Brock's phone vibrated, and Mahalia Borcher, 149 Duck Branch Road, Sneedville, Tennessee 37869, came through. He stuck the phone in Maude's face for her to see the name.

Maude said, "I can't believe that a person would take an item number off an invoice and use it as the portal for an anonymous cryptocurrency account."

Federal marshals arrested the Borchers and Brunnells in Sneedville a week later for the murders of Jalen and Margo Millhouse, and for trying to extort money from Vigneron Winery.

~ ~ ~

The following spring, the hum of an Italian sports car got louder as it approached. Maude pivoted and ran to the door to see if it was Brock Skinner. He came to share the good news with her. He had bought the farm behind the winery from the Millhouse estate and planned to refurbish it.

# THE PROCTOR SHE
# SHED MYSTERY

Muriel Proctor, heiress to the Hennessy copper fortune, angled off Bonds Mill Road through the gentle swale across the front of the property and drove to the stone ruins where the contractor was parked. She launched out of her Land Rover and high-stepped across the overgrown fescue to reach the excavating crew. "Good morning, guys. Need somebody to operate the backhoe?"

Ronald Amick, owner of Branch Bank Construction, said, "Hah. You might get carpal tunnel, and I can't afford any more workman's comp claims."

"What have you got?" She switched instantly to a more serious tone.

Amick walked around to the backside of the large hole and pointed at something in the dirt that looked like a small wooden footlocker. "We hit this. I didn't want to bring it up without you watching."

Muriel bent over the edge and said, "Well, get the thing out of there. Try not to damage it."

Two men climbed down in the hole with shovels and began clearing dirt away from the edges. They pried both ends until it broke free. Amick and the backhoe operator grabbed the box as the two men below hoisted it over their heads. "Where do you want it?"

"In the back of my car," Muriel replied. After the box had been loaded, she said to Ron, "I have a confidentiality agreement with me that I want you to sign." She retrieved it from the Land Rover dash and handed it to him along with a pen. "I'll send you a copy in the mail."

Mort and Muriel Proctor lived in New York City for the eighteen years of their marriage until he dropped dead of a heart attack a year ago. Muriel decided to leave the city for Kentucky's bluegrass because someone told her it was the center of the universe. She bought a penthouse in downtown Lexington and brought her estimable wealth with her, but still had to deal with Mort's collection of burgundy wines back in the city.

Seven months ago, Muriel was on a day trip to Four Roses Distillery with the local gentry when she saw a pasture for sale nearby that had remnants of a primitive structure. Nothing remained but the foundation and a portion of the floor, and visible signs that it had once had a basement, which was now filled in with dirt and covered in thorny brush.

She liked the location of the property. It was right off a Bluegrass Parkway exit, merely twenty-five minutes from her digs in downtown Lexington. It felt like a getaway up the Hudson River in New York without the two-hour train trip. Muriel bought the land and began designing the "she shed" she always wanted. Once the plans were approved, she hired Ronald Amick, who had the necessary experience to complete the project.

Solomon and Humility "Milly" Rigsdale sat in rattan chairs on the side porch of their craftsman-style home in Harrison, New York, waiting for the call to be answered. "Hi, is this Muriel? How are you?" Solomon claimed his ancestors came over on the *Mayflower*, which made him a bona fide blue blood.

"Oh, Sol, it's you. How's Milly?"

"If she was any better, you'd wanna be her."

"Good to hear. Are you just checking up on me?" Muriel asked.

"I wanted to let you know that I'm still interested in buying Mort's wine collection. I'm sure it's been a nuisance, and I'll give you top dollar for it."

"That's very sweet of you, Solomon, but I haven't decided yet what I'm going to do with it."

"Well, fine. When you're ready to sell, please keep me in mind."

"I certainly will." Milly got on the line, and the two women talked for nearly fifteen minutes until the doorman knocked on Muriel's door.

"I broomed the dirt off, ma'am, and here's a piece of plastic to set it on." He shimmied the crate off the dolly onto the tile floor in the entryway. Muriel tipped him a hundred-dollar bill.

The hasp was so rusted that it fell into her hand when she went to raise it. The hinges broke off too, freeing the lid. A solid poplar board rested on top of the contents of the box. She removed it to find six bottles of something underneath. She gently extracted one of them and cradled it in her hands. It was dark green glass. The top had been dipped in black wax. Crudely etched on the glass were the year 1802 and the name Daniel Boone. She checked the box again to see if there was anything else besides the bottles. Handwriting on a yellowed piece of paper said:

*Jean Jacques Dufour,*

*In 1783, I staked the land where you grow grapes. Our family left the United States for the Missouri territory of Louisiana this year only to find wine making to be prohibited here by the mother country. When your wine is available for sale, I would like to purchase all that you have for resale. Given under my hand this 3rd day of Nov. 1799*

*Daniel Boone*

Muriel grinned with excitement and hotfooted it over to the corner window in the living room where her cell phone sat on the side table next to the high-back Queen Anne chair. She looked up a number and placed a call. "Emile? Muriel Proctor. I've come across six bottles of wine that could be over two hundred years old. I need you to authenticate them for me."

Emile replied, "Ah, Muriel, how lovely to hear from you again. Let me have the address where I can pick them up. I will have our people there within hours." Emile Ponsonby's ancestors came into Virginia just before the Revolutionary War, which didn't quite make him a blue blood, but he sure acted like one.

Ponsonby was considered the premier wine authenticator in the world. When Mort Proctor was alive tossing around Muriel's money, buying expensive wines from Burgundy, Emile became the clearinghouse for his purchases. He practically lived off Mort's business until Mort unexpectedly went south of the dirt.

Branch Bank Construction, not surprisingly, specialized in constructing branch banks. Banks had vaults. Amick had the reputation of being able to build impenetrable vaults. Muriel Proctor saw the value in that because she wanted a "Fort Knox" of a wine cellar put in under her she shed. She intended to relocate Mort's five-million-dollar wine collection to Kentucky.

The cellar was poured concrete on all six sides and had a bank-vault door. The inside was lined with cedar racking, floor to ceiling, and the air conditioner that kept the humidity at 55 percent and temperature at fifty-five degrees was mounted high up on the back wall. The stairs up and down had a switchback, and there was a thick oak door at the top leading into the she shed.

When finished, the hexagonal shed had a thirteen-foot vaulted ceiling of distressed blond wood. There was a small shower and toilet by the front door, and the balance of the room was filled with mustard glass-front cabinets full of pots, tools, bibelots, and gewgaws. A rococo worktable stood in the middle of the room with antiqued brown bar chairs all around it. The TV and stereo were inside a big armoire on the wall next to the door to the wine cellar. A refrigerator filled with expensive wines and snacks was tucked under the TV. Arched clerestory windows ran around the tops of the walls to let in natural light.

The confidentiality agreement Amick signed pertained to the security feature Muriel designed. On the back wall, a solid panel was engineered to rise out of the floor, squaring off the corner, leaving a triangular space behind it that would be hard to infiltrate. When the wall was down, there was no evidence of its existence showing on the tile floor. If Muriel felt threatened, she could go to the corner, press a button, the wall would go up, and she could call for help.

The genius of the device, not noticed by others, came from the trompe l'oeil painting done by a Colombian artist who copied the look of the corner behind the wall. The work of art had depth. It sold an illusion to onlookers that they were actually seeing the room's inside corner. Whether the wall was up or down, the eyes were unable to discern the difference.

The exterior of the she shed mimicked the detail of the Four Roses Distillery up the street. The butter-colored plaster and orange tile roof were gilded with dark brown gingerbread under the eaves and gutters. The construction project that began in March was completed in late August, in time to get the wine moved into the cellar before Keeneland's fall meet in October.

Emile Ponsonby had been in possession of Muriel's wine bottles for six months. He finally called to report his findings. "These bottles are from 1802. The vinedresser of First Vineyard, established in 1799, was, in fact, John James Dufour. The winery, located on the banks of the Kentucky River, was the first commercial wine operation in the United States."

"Oh, how fun."

"I have prepared a package of materials documenting their authenticity. We carbon and protein dated the note from Daniel Boone, and then had several handwriting experts affirm his writing style and signature."

"The note from him doesn't necessarily make the wine legitimate. Someone could have placed the real note with some phony wine," she asserted.

"You're right. We also scrutinized the bottles and wax. We compared the shape and color of the bottles against specimens known from that time period, finding an exact match. The wax is also a match, and its chemical composition is correct. These bottles are authentic. No doubt about it."

"What about the wine itself?"

Emile said, "There has been virtually no evaporation. The bottles languished in a cool, dark place for over two hundred years. They have been remarkably preserved."

"Hot damn. What do you think they're worth?" she hooted.

"Oh, I couldn't hazard a guess. Pretty sure each bottle would bring north of a million."

"I don't need the money. Do you think I can feature them in my new wine cellar?" Muriel asked.

"That's a capital idea."

"Wait. Something else comes to mind. How about I give you three of the bottles if you help me on a little project I'm planning?"

"Gladly. Just let me know how I can be of assistance."

"For the time being, send me a bill for your services. I want you to come to visit in October. I'm going to invite Solomon and

Milly Rigsdale to the races, and you can be my escort. We can visit my new wine cellar."

"I accept. Share the date with me as soon as you've completed the arrangements."

In late September, Muriel Proctor made daily trips to her she shed after lunch. She stayed busy potting plants, assembling floral arrangements, and getting ready for company. She had asked Emile Ponsonby to arrive a couple of days before the Rigsdales to critique how Mort's wine collection was being featured in the new cellar. She was also working out every detail of the project that Emile would help her with.

Milly and Solomon knocked on Muriel's door at eleven o'clock on the first Thursday in October. Emile greeted them and ushered the couple into the big living room. "Nice view you have here, Muriel. It ain't what you had in New York, but still nice."

"I agree. It's wonderful to see you folks again. Sol, I hope you're not upset with me keeping the wine collection. After the races, I'll take you out to the new cellar I had built. If you behave, I'll also let you pick out an expensive bottle of wine for us to have at dinner."

"A 2008 La Tache. That's what I've been hankering for," Solomon heralded with a clownish face.

The afternoon at Keeneland ended up being one of the best times all four of them could recall. The weather couldn't have been better. The buffet was delicious, everybody won some money, and it felt good to be with the smart set. The group stood together, waiting for the valet to bring the cars. The Rigsdales had a rental they would drive back to the hotel after dinner. Emile rode with Muriel, and she led the way to the she shed that was only fifteen minutes away.

"Look at this place," Milly blurted dramatically as she neared the little building that reminded her of a Spanish mission.

"Muriel, you've outdone yourself," Solomon added.

"Let's go inside." Muriel keyed open the door and swung it toward her. Once in, she turned on some music and pulled a tray of nibbles out of the refrigerator. "Emile, pick out a smooth white wine and open it." The Rigsdales walked around the perimeter of the shed to see what all was in the cabinets. The six o'clock sun blazed through the windows overhead. After a few minutes, Muriel said, "Follow me. I want to show you the cellar." The four of them stood together at the bottom of the stairs while she opened the vault door. "Take a peek at this."

"I think I've died and gone to heaven," Solomon said as he ran his eyes over the scads of bottles neatly stacked everywhere. He noticed a clear case that housed three old-fashioned wines with etched bottles. "What are these, Muriel?"

"Those are wines produced by the first commercial winery in the United States, which was right here in Kentucky. They belonged to Daniel Boone, but never got to him."

Emile said, "I spent six months checking them out. They're legit."

"Where did you find 'em?" Milly asked.

"Right where we're standing. We unearthed the cases as we were digging the hole for the cellar."

"Some people have all the luck." Solomon's voice lessened. He broke a sweat and began to look pale. "If you'll excuse me, I need to visit the restroom." He struggled a bit to climb the stairs.

Five minutes later, Milly said, "I wonder what's keeping Sol? I hope he's not ill. It's not like him to not want to take in all this wine."

Emile spoke up. "I'll go and check on him." He bounded up the stairs and slammed the door. In around thirty seconds, Ponsonby opened the door and broadcasted, "He's not in the restroom, nor do I see him outside. I don't know what's happened to him."

Swiftly, the women rushed up to search for him. Milly scanned each of the walls. She began to panic. There was no use checking the restroom, so she hurried outside. Nothing.

Muriel yelled from the door, "Milly, the only thing I can think of is that he might have staggered out to the road and hitched a ride to a hospital. There's one in Lawrenceburg. Do you have your car keys?"

"I think they're in it," she said frantically. "How far is the hospital?"

"Ten miles."

Emile said, "I'll take Muriel's car and look for him too." Milly jumped in the rental and jerked it into drive.

Thirty minutes later, she returned crestfallen. "No sign of him."

Muriel declared, "Let's call the police."

It was getting dark when the two officers arrived. For the next hour, every detail of the evening was reviewed and discussed. The police took down the addresses and phone numbers of everybody in the group. One of the officers asked Milly, "Ma'am, how long do you think Mr. Ponsonby was up here checking on your husband?"

"No more than thirty seconds."

"And how long was your husband upstairs before he checked on him?"

"About five minutes."

The officer said, "So, it seems that one of two things might have happened. When Mr. Rigsdale went upstairs, he either left on his own or was taken away, or when Mr. Ponsonby went to look for him, he hid the body somewhere and disposed of it when you went to check the hospital."

Muriel commented, "That's macabre. How and where could Emile hide a body in less than thirty seconds? He's never even been here before."

"Not likely," said the policeman. "It isn't relevant until we find a body. We'll treat it as a missing person's case for now. He'll likely turn up in the next day or so with an explanation."

The two officers went outside. Before they got in their car, the other policeman said to Muriel, "If you'll let me have a key, I'll send some men over here in the morning to look around."

The late dinner that Muriel, Emile, and Milly had was somber. They went their separate ways at ten o'clock when the steak house began to close.

Milly called Muriel midmorning and said, "I haven't heard a thing. If you don't mind, I'd like to go back out to your shed and take another look around."

"Sure, I'll pick you up at your hotel in half an hour."

Muriel walked into her she shed ahead of Milly and threw her keys on the table in the middle of the room. Milly put it right out there. "So, did you know that Mort and I had an affair?"

"Why, Milly, how on earth would I have known that?"

"I don't know, but I think you killed him because of it. I'm going to ask the police to exhume his body and check to see if you poisoned him."

"That won't work. I had his body cremated."

Milly became angry and spoke sternly. "Then I think you poisoned Sol to get back at me. I can't believe that Emile Ponsonby would help you kill my husband."

"Emile is a classy man. We're to be married," Muriel admitted smugly. "There he is now." The sound of a car approaching could be heard outside.

"Where have you taken my husband's body?"

"The same place we're going to take yours." Emile stepped through the door and leaned on the wall with a supercilious grin on his face.

Suddenly, the trompe l'oeil panel began to lower into the floor. One of the policemen from last night was standing behind it with his revolver in hand. He strolled over to Emile and said, "Now I know how you did it. You drugged him with wine, dragged his body behind this panel, and then hauled him off while Mrs. Rigsdale went to the hospital."

Muriel's body language was subdued. "How did you find the panel?" she asked.

"I had our men x-ray the floor this morning."

"Officer, could I interest you in a bottle of wine once owned by Daniel Boone? It's worth at least a million dollars."

"Are you trying to bribe me?" the policeman asked. At that moment, Milly charged Muriel and began choking her barehanded. Emile ran out the door and tried unsuccessfully to escape.

When the officer returned to his desk at the station, he logged onto his computer and made a stick-on label for the case file folder that read: PROCTOR SHE SHED MYSTERY – SOLVED.

# A CRIME OF PASTA PASSION

## TWO YEARS AND THREE MONTHS AGO

At four o'clock on a frigid Thursday afternoon in January, tiny sleet balls glanced off the iced-up picture window of Nicastro's on Kenmare Street in Little Italy. The restaurant, renowned for its pastas and sauces, was gearing up for the daily onslaught of New York City foodies who would brave the cold to stand in line for a table starting at 5:15.

Elia Nicastro used his apron to dry his hands, came out of the kitchen, and stated to his wife, "Join me in the office for a minute." He went around behind his desk and waited for Martina to seat herself across from him. "I'm selling the restaurant," he said, just like that.

She clenched the arms of the chair, flared her elbows, and replied, "Why in the world would you do that? The business is incredibly successful." Her face became a blend of contempt and confusion.

"It'll never be more valuable, and besides, there are easier ways to make a living than working ten hours a day, seven days a week." Elia leaned back in his comfortable wicker chair, rubbed his chin, and looked away.

"But what about the girls?" she probed. "This has been their whole life."

"I'm ready to leave the city. With the money we get for this place, the children can do whatever they want. If we had a son who could take over, I would consider keeping it, but we don't."

Martina stood and deliberately walked to the closet to retrieve her mink coat. After she put it on, buttoned it, and gyrated her body to twist the alpaca scarf around her neck, a loathsome expression accompanied her proclamation, "So, it's my fault."

"I'm not saying that."

"You don't have to." She left the office and marched through the dining room, out the front door, onto the ice-covered sidewalk, never to set foot in the restaurant again.

## LATER THAT YEAR

Martina still wasn't speaking to Elia after the sale of Nicastro's for six million dollars. The children were given remunerative one-year employment contracts, and incessantly talked about what they would do when their tour of duty at the establishment they helped build ended.

Elia had been looking for the perfect place to relocate to for nearly a year. He finally found it on Friday after Thanksgiving, a redbrick farmhouse with acreage and a fairly new concrete building that sat back from the highway, on Avenstoke Road in Waddy, a vapid town in the dead center of Kentucky. Martina begrudgingly joined him before Christmas when they took possession of the remote property. The plan was to repurpose the outbuilding as the kitchen for pastas and sauces.

## LAST FRIDAY NIGHT

Domenico "Dom" Lamberti was on top of the world on Good Friday a year ago. He fell off it a few days later when Titian Red opened its doors the Thursday after Easter. Dom's posh white-tablecloth bistro, Veneziano, on Louisville's Whiskey Row, had once been considered the finest Italian food spot in Kentucky. Not anymore. Titian Red dethroned it almost instantly.

Dom said to the host, "I have a reservation under the name of Rice." A voluptuous hostess in a tight black dress seated him at a two-top in the corner against the wall. The waiter strolled over and made pleasantries before handing Dom the menus and wine list. One menu had traditional Italian favorites, and the other was dedicated to pastas and sauces. The pasta dishes were what people came to Titian Red to eat, accompanied by the unusual "natural" wine offerings.

While Dom Lamberti waited to place his order, he took in the establishment's atmosphere. The high walls had been done in a mustard stucco. There were copies of paintings by Titian, mostly of the woman with red hair, hung randomly, conveying feminine charm. The pasta menu, black print on yellow thatch paper, had been done in a folksy style, appropriate for a rustic Italian dining experience.

*Pick Your Type and Size of Pasta*
*Plain Egg Angel Hair (1/16")*
*Lemon Pepper Spaghetti (1/8")*
*Black Pepper Linguine (1/4")*
*Whole Wheat Fettuccini (3/8")*
*Spinach Wide Fettuccini (1/2")*
*Basil Pappardelle (3/4")*
*Mushroom Wide Pappardelle (1")*
*Rosemary Lasagna (3")*

*Choose a Complementary Sauce*
*Maria's Mushroom Walnut*
*Anna's Tomato Basil*
*Rosa's Alfredo*
*Teresa's Pesto*
*Elena's White Clam*

*Angela's Bolognese*
*Carmela's Marinara*
*Lucia's Arrabbiata*

Dom selected the lemon-pepper fettuccini with Alfredo sauce. It was the absolute best he had ever tasted. When the check came, he queried, "Is the pasta and sauce made on the premises?"

The waiter played coy, saying, "I'm not sure, sir." That meant the answer was no. Lamberti paid the bill and ducked out quickly, hoping patrons that might know him from Veneziano wouldn't recognize him.

He reverse-engineered the work schedule at Titian Red on the car ride home. It opened at five and closed at ten, which meant the staff worked an eight-hour day, from three until eleven. The restaurant would be cleaned from three to four, and food deliveries would stream in until five as the cooks prepped for every dish on the menu.

Lamberti sat in his company car on the next afternoon like a cheap gumshoe, watching trucks pull up and away from the loading dock behind Titian Red. A blue Mercedes box van appeared to be the vehicle transporting pastas and sauces, so he dropped in behind it onto the I-64 ramp heading east. Forty minutes and forty-seven miles later, the van exited at Highway 151 to the south, toward Lawrenceburg. It pulled into an uphill driveway just across the Anderson County line, under an archway that read "Terroir Winery."

The van parked in the back, and Dom wheeled into the lot for visitors. The sign next to the double-door front entrance read "Open 9-6 Tues thru Sat." The troweled-on tawny plaster over concrete block was broken up by honey-yellow windows and maroon shutters. Red tulips clustered at the base of the building had just bloomed. The ivy and wisteria were poised to crawl up the wall as the weather warmed. Striped rows of grapevines along the driveway and at the side and rear of the winery were deplorably uninspiring. Dom stepped into the tasting room to check the place out at a little past five o'clock.

"Would you like to try some of our wines?" the man at the end of the bar inquired. There were rows of bottles with different titles on the homespun shelves above him.

Dom said, "You know, I think I saw this brand at Titian Red in Louisville last night."

"Why, yes. They pretty much buy up everything we can make. My name's Renato Ferrante. People call me Renny. My wife and I are the owners." He pointed at a picture of himself and his wife, smiling, locked in a warm embrace.

"Well, from one Italian to another, I'm Domenico Lamberti. I go by Dom." They shook hands.

"Are you a natural wine fan?" Renny pulled a bottle of Zinfandel down as an exemplar.

"I don't know that much about them," Dom replied, a bald-faced lie.

Renny didn't believe him and responded, "Oh, I doubt that. People don't come here unless they are looking for the raw product." He served a small cluster of samples and explained the natural process, which meant the use of organic grapes, indigenous or wild yeast, with nothing added or taken away. He did admit that the grapes were shipped in from an organic farm in California.

Dom sipped off the last one and said, "These are quite good. I think I'm becoming a fan. Nice meeting you." Renny nodded and waved to him. Dom had satisfied himself that pastas and sauces were not being made at this location.

On the way out, he noticed a package of fresh noodles and a tub of sauce in the cooler, both with handmade black-and-white labels that read "Eight Sisters Pastas and Sauces." He remembered that Titian Red offered eight choices, each with a woman's appellation. "Where are these from?" he asked.

Renny looked up and said, "Oh, some ladies that live around here bring it to my wife from time to time. Give it a try. It's pretty good stuff."

"I think I will. Can you get more if I really like it?" He tossed a twenty onto the bar.

"I'm not sure. I'll have to ask the boss." He pointed this time to a different picture of his bride informally tacked up next to the door that led to the backroom.

Dom tramped into his restaurant's kitchen at seven o'clock and gave instructions to the corpulent head chef to heat up the pasta meal he held in his hand. It looked like pappardelle and Bolognese. He insisted the cook taste it when it was ready. "This stuff is magnificent! Where did you get it?"

"I'm not sure." Dom presented his hands, palms up.

"How can you not be sure? Did this come from Titian Red?"

"Not exactly." He took a fork and twirled the pappardelle with sauce on it and maneuvered the bite into his mouth. "Damn, that's good. I think the pasta has rosemary in it." Dom frowned at the plate of food, threw the fork down, and exited the kitchen with a sense of injury.

He walked into Titian Red at eight o'clock sharp that Saturday night, asked if he could place a to-go order and get a drink while he waited. The hostess smiled politely and threw her hand to the right. Dom told the man behind the bar that he wanted the rosemary pappardelle topped with Bolognese. "Also, could you pour me a glass of wine from the Terroir Winery? Zinfandel if you have it." The bartender got the proper stemware and filled it half full. "Say, can you tell me why this place is called Titian Red?" Dom asked.

"Titian was a famous sixteenth-century Italian painter. He did a lot of portraits of women with red hair, like what's hanging all around here." He glanced up at the wall for half a second. "The eight sisters that own the place have reddish-blonde hair. Their family used to own a restaurant in New York City by the name of Nicastro's. There's one of the sisters." He peeked up again, and Dom turned around to see to whom he referred. She was younger than he would have thought and stunningly beautiful.

"And I'm guessing their names are tied to the eight items on the sauce menu."

The bartender smiled and said, "You got it, man."

When Dom sat at his dining room table at home just after nine o'clock, he inhaled the pasta dish like a trencherman going to the electric chair. His wife, Ghita, glared at him as though he was a man possessed.

Lamberti spent all Sunday morning reading everything he could find on the Internet about the restaurant the Nicastro family had built and sold. He called a private detective to say, "I need you to find where Elia and Martina Nicastro live. They have to be somewhere here in Kentucky."

Renny Ferrante's wife dedicated Sunday afternoon to taking a detailed inventory at the winery. Later that day, she joined the Nicastro family at the commissary for the weekly meeting, which included the eight sisters. The luscious, pervasive smell of garlic and savory spices used in the pasta sauces heightened everyone's supper appetite. Martina Nicastro began the meeting with, "Last week, I made improvements to your father's office in the house. I had a better sound system put in for him." The women sniggered tacitly. "So, this week, Maria, Teresa, Angela, and Carmela will do the cooking on Monday through Wednesday, and then Anna, Rosa, Elena, and Lucia can step in Thursday to Saturday. It's Renny's turn to drive the van back and forth for the week. Soon we're going to have to address running out of the natural wines." The rest of the meeting turned into a free-for-all on the wine topic that ended without any resolution.

The women ambled over to the farmhouse when it was supper-time to take their normal seats at the craftsman-style dining room table that had been in the New York City house. Elia's spot was at one end next to his wife, Martina. Renny rushed in a few minutes later and took the seat at the other end, just in time for the blessing. Renny declared after the meal, "A suspicious guy by the name of Dom Lamberti came into the winery yesterday inquiring about the pasta we had for sale in the cooler. He bought it and asked if we could get more. I'm not so sure selling extra stuff you guys make is a good idea. I checked the security camera, and his vanity plate read Veneziano."

Martina Nicastro replied, "I knew that name sounded familiar. He's the guy that owns an Italian restaurant right up the street from us in Louisville. We can't afford to have him find the kitchen. Could blow things wide open. We don't need to deal with that right now."

~ ~ ~

The detective called on Monday at midday to report that the Nicastros lived at 18955 Avenstoke Road, Waddy, Kentucky. Dom recalled Renny Ferrante at Terroir Winery had told him the pastas were made by women who lived nearby.

## TUESDAY

The Greeks consider Tuesday to be unlucky because it was the day of the week Constantinople fell. The Spanish don't like it either. Tuesday and the planet Mars share the same astrological symbol. Mars was the god of war, therefore, all about death. For the Greeks and Spaniards, a Tuesday is particularly unlucky if it falls on the thirteenth of the month, which it did on that damp April morning in Kentucky.

Dom found a place to park before sunup on the side of the road where he could watch cars and trucks entering and leaving the purported residence of Elia and Martina Nicastro. He had a clear view of the redbrick farmhouse, but didn't see the outbuilding among the budding trees at the back of the property.

The sisters on cooking duty were in the kitchen, ready to start their eight-hour shifts. The day began by placing ingredients for the sauces next to the pots and burners to be used. Each cook was responsible for two sauces. Elia Nicastro had perfected the recipes over the last thirty years. Once the sauces were going, all four sisters switched to making pastas, working as a team around the big rolling and cutting machine. Everything got packaged up at the loading dock by two thirty. The van was securely loaded by three with wines added on the back, and then down the road it would go.

Dom had been sitting in his car for eight hours and hadn't seen a single vehicle enter or leave the Nicastro property. He became impatient and at two forty-five pulled out onto the main road and into the driveway leading up to the redbrick farmhouse. Martina Nicastro saw him turn in and quickly made a phone call. "Lamberti is driving up to the house."

"See if you can get rid of him. If I don't hear back from you in ten minutes, I'll pull over there in the van."

Martina flipped a switch on the wall and answered the door.

"Hello, ma'am. My name's Dom Lamberti. I have an Italian restaurant in Louisville. I was hoping that you and your husband would consider selling me some of your recipes. I saw online where they are considered the best in the world." He heard booming conversation coming through a closed door off the hall, just inside the front door. "You are Martina Nicastro, aren't you?"

"I am. You'll have to come back later. My husband is on an important conference call right now and can't be disturbed." Then more intermittent talk could be heard spouting from behind the door.

"When would be convenient?" he asked politely.

"Give me your phone number, and I'll call and let you know if my husband is interested in seeing you." There was silence for a few seconds, and then conversation in the other room started up again. Dom pulled a calling card out and handed it to her, preparing to leave. She took the card and eased the door shut in his face. Flipping off the switch, she went to join her husband in his office. Dom turned back and saw Martina through the sheers in the front window. Her husband, Elia, was holding a phone to his ear with his back to her.

When Dom began to get in his car, he remembered something troubling. He looked toward the front window again and saw that she was gone. Dom quietly re-latched the car door and snuck around to the right side of the farmhouse. He squinted to look through the window to see if Elia Nicastro was still sitting there. What Lamberti saw was a dressed-up mannequin with a gaping grimace and phone next to its ear.

Dom ran to the back corner of the farmhouse in time to see the blue Mercedes van pull away from a building tucked in the trees at the back of the property. It was heading in his direction. He looked again across the open field and could see the Terroir Winery building on the land abutting the rear of the Nicastro property.

Renny Ferrante saw Dom Lamberti turn and run in the direction of his car, so he pulled the van to the front of the house and parked it before Dom could get there. Renny reached in the glove box, pulled out a pistol, hopped to the ground, and slammed the van door.

"Oh, Renny," Lamberti said with labored breathing. "What's going on?"

"Dom, you should have minded your own business."

"I was until I remembered that Martina Nicastro is the same woman that you showed me to be your wife in those pictures at the winery." He took a few steps closer to his car and kept talking. "What, did you kill Elia and take his wife? That building back there must be where the pastas and sauces are made for Titian Red, am I right?"

"Elia wouldn't let the girls use his recipes. So, we all kind of agreed. He had to go. He treated Martina like garbage after she gave him eight beautiful girls. He wanted a boy. I guess he should have had a family vote before selling the restaurant. It would have saved his life. And yours." Renny shot Dom Lamberti right through the forehead and got back in the van to drive the food and wine to Titian Red. He figured Martina and the girls would clean up the mess just as they'd done when he popped Elia.

Renny rolled down the van window to smell the honeysuckle rising up in the air as he turned onto Avenstoke Road toward Louisville.

# A Fungus Among Us

Lisa Mae Kryer continued washing goblets behind the stainless-steel bar at the tasting room of her charming little wine operation as she giddily laughed at the sublime proclamations of Leonard Howe and Orin Withers. The men were munching fresh lemon fungi salads, doused with parmesan vinaigrette, made from mushrooms grown indoors, right up the street from Kryer Cellars, on the same side of Lexington Road and the other side of the cemetery.

Leonard said, "There are eight billion people in the world, two and a half billion Christians, two billion Muslims, one and a half billion Hindus, one billion Buddhists, Jews, and people of other religions, and one billion atheists. Only one of those groups has it right, which means most people in the world have it wrong. That's proof enough that a majority opinion on anything can't be trusted."

Orin's circumspect response was "That reminds me... Woody Hayes said when you pass the football, only three things can happen and two of them are bad. The same goes for dying. You either go up, down, or nowhere, and two of those things are bad as well. I'm going with the Christians. They're a majority when independently compared to each of the other groups. That's how you have to look at it."

"Bosh," Leonard retorted, dismissing his partner out of hand. The two men looked at Lisa Mae as if she were the arbiter of the argument. Leonard said, "Do you agree that the correct way to pick the best wine in a contest is to have an elimination where you take the top two and vote again to determine a winner?"

Orin piped up, "Before you answer, Lisa Mae, consider this. If everyone had to choose between Christianity and Islam, it's possible the Hindus would throw in with the Muslims for political reasons, making Islam the winner, with fewer original followers than Christianity."

"Guys, I don't know. All I know is that if they tell me my wine's the best, I'll take their word for it," she said apologetically. Kryer Cellars reds had been entered in the Best Wines in America competition to be held next week in New Orleans. Lisa Mae, invited to submit a wine to be judged, paid the substantial entrance fee and shipped off several bottles, ready to take on the heavyweights. She was doing so because every oenophile who came by said her wines were the best they'd ever tasted. Blind luck on her part, she figured, but might as well find out for sure.

Rose Face Fungi, by the south edge of the cemetery, was the foremost commercial cultivator of mushrooms in the world. Owners Leonard Howe and Orin Withers discovered how to grow a fungus normally only found in the wild heretofore, namely, the matsutake mushroom that sold for $400 a pound in Japan. The two men also had the secrets for producing shitakes, maitakes, hedgehogs, blewits, puffballs, oysters, enokis, creminis, armillarias, portabellas, porcinis, chanterelles, cordyceps, and turkey tails, and knew how to grow the "death cap," a deadly poisonous fungus, as well as psilocybin, the oft-consumed hallucinogenic "magic shrooms," which were illegal until Colorado changed their laws.

Sixty billion dollars' worth of mushrooms were consumed annually worldwide; what the Japanese call umami, the fifth taste category of meat or broth that goes along with the other four profiles of sweet, sour, salty, and bitter, making fungi a natural meat substitute for satisfying a particular taste craving. Howe and Withers were selling all they could grow, making a bunch of money. When Lisa Mae came to them with the idea of adding food at her winery, "Frick and Frack," as they were called, suggested she feature dishes with mushrooms, so she did. It had been a roaring success.

Kryer Cellars, west of Lexington Road and north of the cemetery in Danville, Kentucky, was hands down the most beautiful and immaculate spread for miles around. Lisa Mae was serious about simplicity and order. She was constantly cleaning the place with microfiber cloths, hot water, and vinegar. Her disposition, angelic while at work, had a spiritual quality. There was never any clutter, and her clothes (she was partial to Retrofete Ada black denim jackets) were always clean and pressed. Her favorite book, *The Life-Changing Magic of Tidying Up* by Marie Kondo, became her organizer. The only thing freeform around the place was the modern art strategically placed on the eggplant-colored walls of the eatery.

The footprint of the Kryer Cellars building was a shoe box—narrow and deep. The front, two-story façade had honey-colored siding, lime-green shutters, and white columns, corners, and fascia. Four narrow dormers were perched on the metal roof. The parking lot and access road to the winery proper were on the graveyard side. The outdoor seating on the veranda along the north face of the building overlooked a horse farm and rows of grapevines. The back two-thirds of the structure was brick veneer, painted to match the front, broken up by rows of small windows.

Lisa Mae hadn't been able to attend the Best Wines in America competition because she had no one to cover for her. Two weeks after she sent her reds to be judged, a red Porsche wheeled into Kryer's lot at lunchtime and parked near the front door. A man wearing a charcoal gray suit with white thread and baby-blue four-in-hand necktie locked the Porsche and entered the winery. The hostess seated him at a table near the tasting-room bar. Lisa Mae handed the man a menu and asked, "Can I get you a glass of wine?"

"Yes, thank you. One of your reds, please. By the way, do you know if Miss Kryer is here today?"

"Call me Lisa Mae. Everybody does."

"Nice to make your acquaintance, ma'am. My name's Davey Moore," he said attentively. "I'm from Best Wines in America, and I've got some good news for you."

"Yes?"

"Kryer Cellars red has won the double gold, best in show."

She looked over at the next table and said, "Did you hear that, guys?"

Leonard and Orin said in unison, "We heard it." Orin added, "Congratulations!"

She turned back to Moore and said, "I can't believe it. Thank you, thank you. This is incredible."

Moore replied, "You're very welcome. After I have some lunch, I'll bring in the award, and you can tell me your secret."

Leonard butted in, saying, "Get the tofu soup and ham sandwich."

"Sounds good," Moore acquiesced. Lisa Mae brought the bowl of soup, a spoon, and saucer, and set them on the table. He sipped a spoonful and said, "Wow, this is delicious."

"Distilled water, mushroom powder, tofu, salt, and scallions," Orin reported. "Leonard and I make the powder right up the street."

"Oh, really?" Moore was starting to wonder if the two men were crackpots.

"Yeah, we grow all kinds of mushrooms indoors."

Lisa Mae came with the ham sandwich. Leonard and Orin were courteous enough to go vocally dormant.

"I'm not sure I've ever seen such a beautiful winery, and you definitely make spectacular wine."

"Oh, thank you," she said.

Once done with lunch, Davey Moore went to his car to fetch the ribbons and plaques that came with being a champion oenologist. He set everything on the tasting-room bar and said, "The wine press will learn of the results of our competition tomorrow, so get ready to be inundated with calls from people wanting to buy every bottle you have. My advice is for you to raise your prices as soon as I leave."

"I will, and thank you again." She beamed a smile of euphoria.

"Now, if you'll be kind enough to quickly walk me through your operation and let me take a couple of pictures, I'll get out of your hair." Twenty minutes later, Moore said pleasantries and headed for his car. He heard someone speaking at him as he fobbed open the doors of his Porsche.

Leonard and Orin were standing by a pickup truck farther out in the lot. Leonard was saying, "Come over to our place, and we'll tell you the secret for making good wine."

Moore turned to face the men and said, "Beg your pardon?"

"We know how to make great wine," Orin declared. "Follow us to our place, and we'll show you."

Being somewhat disinterested in touring an indoor mushroom growing operation, Moore feigned enthusiasm as the three of them went through the door in the office leading to the fetid shop. Leonard remarked, "Sorry about the smell. We've gotten used to it."

"This place is incredible. Are all of these different mushrooms edible?"

"With a couple of exceptions," Orin stated. They walked down the aisle a little farther. Orin pointed and said, "This baby is known as a death cap. Poisonous."

"What happens if you eat it?"

"Oh, several hours later, you get stomach cramps, start vomiting, and have diarrhea, like you've got food poisoning, which you have, actually. Then you die, unless you get a liver transplant."

"Why do you grow them?"

"Believe it or not, there is a commercial market for the amatoxins," Leonard revealed. "This mushroom over here may be more to your liking."

Orin said, "Psilocybin. Magic mushrooms. Hallucinogenic."

"No, thanks." The men went through the door leading to the shipping dock where the sweet air was more agreeable. "So, tell me your secret."

"Right here." Orin put his hand on a stack of medium-sized bags piled like a Jenga game. "Mushroom powder. You put a bag of this in a vat for every three thousand gallons of wine must or pulp."

"You're kidding. What kind of mushrooms?"

Leonard fired back, "That we can't tell you."

"How many people know about this?"

"Lisa Mae next door is the only one. And now you know. We're hoping you'll secretly sell this stuff to wineries all over the world as a fermentation additive, not letting anybody know it's mushroom powder."

Davey Moore pondered the situation for five seconds, and then said, "Help me load a few bags in my car."

The harvest season for this year's grapes was nearly over by Halloween, and it had been a wild ride for Lisa Mae since the world learned of her exceptional wines. People showed up in vans wanting to buy and load up everything she had in the cellar. Each customer was limited to one case to get the product out to the widest possible audience. Orders for next year's production were already sold out. Profits were taking off, and so were the number of male suitors pitching every line in the book to attract Lisa Mae's attention.

The tables in the eatery were full at lunchtime. Sunshine at high noon on the Indian-summer day shot through the windows at an angle, checkering the room with patches of light. Each customer chomped away on their mushroom-centric entrees. Lisa Mae looked out at the cemetery and saw a man with a farmer's tan bouncing a small backhoe down the center road, toward the new section over the hill in the back, behind the existing graves. She turned to check on the hungry lunch guests working on their second courses.

~ ~ ~

Davey Moore stepped through the door of the food laboratory in San Francisco where he had dropped off a sample of the mushroom powder for analysis four weeks ago. The technician handed him a report and said, "It's porcini, and not a common version of it. As a matter of fact, the chemical composition indicates that the mushrooms were given some sort of superfood, but I can't really tell what it was."

"That's interesting. What would a superfood be?"

"Some obscure soil that was nutrient rich," he replied cryptically.

"How much do I owe you?" The tech handed him an invoice and returned to his work.

After several weeks of waiting to hear from Davey Moore, Leonard Howe was fuming. "That blasted crook in the red Porsche hasn't called us once since he left here."

"Dollars to donuts, he took our stuff to a lab, trying to figure out what it is," Orin said.

"If he comes around again, we'll square things with him." Speak of the devil, Davey Moore slipped quietly through the front door of Rose Face Fungi. Leonard and Orin jumped up and marched out to accost him. "Why haven't you called us?" Leonard asked.

"I went to a place in Napa Valley to get them to add your kickapoo joy powder to several of their vats. I convinced Reggie Newlin at Zota Winery to try it, so now we'll wait until the spring to see if the stuff works."

"It works. We're not too happy with the way you've handled this. Did you try to find out what the powder is?"

"Yeah, I took it to a lab," Moore admitted.

"You're fired, and if you utter a word about our product to anybody, we'll make sure you get a taste of that death cap I showed you," Leonard warned.

"Hold on now, guys. I know more wineries around the world than anybody else in this business. I need to confirm the fairy dust is legit before I put my reputation on the line."

Orin looked at Leonard warily and then at Moore again. He said, "Forget it, partner. Remember what we said about keeping your mouth shut." Moore, dumbstruck, returned to his car. After he pulled out, Leonard ran to the pickup truck to follow him.

The next morning, the man with the farmer's tan who maintained the cemetery stood in the lobby of the police station, waiting to speak to an officer. When one came out to greet him, he announced, "Someone has buried something at the back of the graveyard without my permission. You can barely see where the ground has been disturbed. I know every inch of that property, and just happened to notice it when I was making the rounds this morning. It must have happened last night."

The policeman urged, "Well, let's go over there and dig it up and see what's down there."

The cemetery attendant, who also dug the graves, began scraping away the dirt with his little backhoe. Not more than three feet down, he hit a wooden box. He jumped off the machine, grabbed a shovel to scrape the soil away from the edge of the lid. He took a crowbar and started prying the box open. When the top sprang loose, he flipped it off. The body inside was face down. It was Lisa Mae Kryer. The policeman got on his radio. "Captain, you better get over here. We've got a dead body. It appears to be the lady that owned the winery next door. I think we're looking for at least two people. I don't believe one person could have managed it."

Her death was big news, especially since she had just gained national notoriety for her Kryer wines. The town of Danville became a mecca for crime solvers and wine snobs alike. Tongues were wagging all around. Leonard Howe and Orin Withers knew who did it, but weren't saying. They had a score to settle with the rakes.

The weather on Sunday after Thanksgiving had turned cold. Leonard and Orin took two different direct flights from Cincinnati to San Francisco using fake names and IDs. They rented a car, drove up to Napa Valley, and checked into separate hotels under their assumed names. Late in the day on Monday, just before closing time, they entered Zota Winery. The place had emptied out. Orin said to the California girl at the tasting bar, "Is Reggie Newlin here?"

"Sure, I'll get him." She went through the door to the winery, returning shortly to report that he would be right up.

Reggie Newlin looked like a buttoned-down accountant, with short, curly hair. He had on a white long-sleeve shirt, olive tie, and dark brown wool slacks. He asked insouciantly, "What can I do for you?"

Leonard said, "We're hoping you can help us locate Davey Moore. We understand he gave you an additive to try in your winemaking process."

"And who are you?"

"Orin Withers. This is Leonard Howe. We're the supplier of the additive."

"I've not heard from him in a while. But since you're here, let me show you our wine operation." He looked over to the girl at the bar and said, "You can take off, Becky. I'll lock up.

"Here are the fermenters." There were four rows of four, all sitting on see-through bar grating. The basement underneath looked to be fifteen feet deep. It was a concrete vault with absolutely nothing in it. "I put the powder in four of these so we could evaluate the effect of the additive against our standard wine."

"What's the basement down there for?" Orin asked.

"Come on, I'll show you." They went down a stairwell with a switchback that led to a solid, hollow-metal door. Newlin opened it and ushered the men through. Once they were all the way in the basement, he stayed in the stairwell, slamming the door behind them. Leonard and Orin glanced at each other and then at the smooth concrete walls. Leonard, in a panic, yelled, "Hey, what's going on?"

Reggie Newlin was now standing above them on the bar grating. "Do you fellows know what happens during the fermentation process?" He stared down at them, hands in his pockets.

"Vaguely," Orin answered lamely.

"When the sugars are converted to alcohol, carbon dioxide is given off."

"I know that much," Leonard replied as he began to see if there was any way out.

"Did you know that carbon dioxide is heavier than air, and it sinks to the bottom of a room?"

"Then get us out of here!" Orin screamed.

Suddenly, Davey Moore came into view. He said, "It's about time you guys came around. We've been waiting for you. In a couple of minutes, you'll go to sleep and never wake up again." He walked away while Reggie Newlin stood and stared at them with a devilish grin.

"You bastards killed Lisa Mae, didn't you? Orin, get on my shoulders and see if you can jump up and grab one of those pipes from the fermenters." They feebly attempted a circus act, to no avail. The pipes were too high in the air. All Orin could think of was whether he was going up, down, or nowhere when he died. He knew he would have to go up if he was to ever see Lisa Mae Kryer again.

Davey Moore pulled keys from Orin Withers' pocket after he passed out. Newlin cleaned out the vehicle and returned it to the San Francisco Airport rental car facility.

After Howe and Withers had been missing for two weeks, they became prime suspects in the killing of Lisa Mae Kryer. The Danville police detective found where the men had traveled to San Francisco under false names, but the trail went dead there. Everyone assumed they left the country. On the last day of the year, Rose Face Fungi was closed down. The assets went up for auction in the spring. Davey Moore bought them for a song.

The attorney representing Lisa Mae's estate was evaluating purchase offers for Kryer Cellars by summertime.

Later in the year, a Zota Winery red won the double gold at the Best Wines in America competition. There wasn't much doubt where Davey Moore and Reggie Newlin were going when they passed on someday. They were going down.

# THE ELUSIVE TOM SMITH

Trevor Donahue was a remarkable IT student at Henderson Community College, so much so, his professors routinely told him he should have gone to MIT or the like where he could have been challenged intellectually. He didn't look very smart. He looked like a hooligan. That's probably why he turned out like he did.

Henderson, Kentucky, across the Ohio River from Evansville, Indiana, had a glorious past, but as river towns go, its best days were in the rearview mirror. Young people came to Henderson with dreams of making a go of a business based on enthusiasm. There just weren't enough people, and even more damning, wasn't enough money around to parlay the downstroke on a charming line of work into something worth the effort. Except in the case of Trevor Donahue. He started a collision repair business right out of college, and before you knew it, he was wearing fancy clothes, driving a Maserati, and hadn't even turned thirty yet.

Minnie Dixon and Sondra Pickering apparently knew how to beat the odds as well. Seven years ago, about the same time Donahue hung out his shingle, the roommates from the University of Louisville opened a winery by the name of Baryla Vineyards, LLC, seven miles due east of downtown Henderson. Trevor wasn't quite sure which of the two women he was trying to woo, but truth be known, he'd take whichever one showed any interest in him. So far, neither had. That didn't keep him from showing up for two glasses of wine most days at five thirty.

Baryla was impressive, a Portuguese fazenda of brown and gray stone with a red terra cotta roof and boatload of black iron trim. The windows were set off by slatted, tawny shutters, and the massive arched double doors of natural wood were a little hard to open because of their heft. The establishment had an inside bar with tables and chairs, and an outside patio that overlooked the scraggly grapevines and rolling hills carpeted with tasseled field corn. The grapes mashed into wine came from all over the world. The back of the bar was lined with bottles that had award ribbons draped on them, a testament to the vintner's quality.

"Trev, do you remember the guy that used to come in occasionally and sit right over there?" Minnie pointed to the table in the corner.

He pivoted to look at the empty chairs. "Yeah. Seemed like an oddball. What was his name?"

"Tom Smith."

"Tom Smith? That's a phony name, like John Doe or something," Donahue remarked.

"He hasn't been here in a month. Wonder what happened to him?" Minnie asked rhetorically. Donahue knew precisely what. Smith was scraping along the bottom of the Ohio River right now, dead.

Trevor built his body shop with a basement and private gate at the end of Beyob Carthom Road. A scissor lift in the last bay went down instead of up, surreptitiously taking vehicles to the lower level. The basement was where all the money was made. The shop, like many others, had deals with big insurance companies for repair work done on the main floor, but no one got rich fixing those cars. The insurance companies made sure of that. The basement was a chop shop where parts were harvested, and cars were rebuilt with stolen components.

Trevor would buy a stripped-down, wrecked, or flooded vehicle at an auto auction for $500 to $1,000 that had a clean title. A car of the same model and color was "located" in St. Louis and brought to the shop in a box truck. Those with tracking devices that couldn't be turned off were left alone. The brought-in ride got stripped within hours. Parts for the purchased vehicle were set aside, and ones not needed were traded or sold to brokers. The parts easy to sell were tires, wheels, bucket seats, airbags, sound systems, catalytic converters, engines, and transmissions. The carcass was taken in the box truck to a scrapyard where it was discreetly disposed of the next day.

One house dealt in body parts such as grills, bumpers, fenders, hoods, doors, and trunks. It was a legitimate business by the name of Tom Smith Automotive, but had its shady side, much the same as Donahue's operation. At first, Smith paid artificially high prices for parts, luring in chop shop operators.

No person by the name of Tom Smith had ever been seen at Tom Smith Automotive, and no one knew why the business bore that name. Trevor, because he was really smart, was the first person to figure out what was going on. He did so after his shop sold stolen parts to Smith, and the shakedown began with threats of exposure. Once Smith was sure the seller was a chop shop, the quid pro quo, of course, was to sell the parts to them at a deep discount in exchange for anonymity. Several weeks ago, Donahue determined the only answer to the problem was to cut off the head of the snake, and quit doing business with Smith.

"Do you want me to see if I can find out what became of your friend, Mister Smith?" Trevor asked.

Sondra Pickering overheard the conversation and spoke before Minnie could answer. "I bet he just got tired of our wines and moved on."

"I doubt that," Trevor replied casually.

"Well, if you run across him around town, let us know," Minnie said.

Smith advertised that they bought used body parts for top prices. If a shop had something to sell, they would go on the website and put in a request for a visit from a buyer who would show up in a truck, pay cash, and haul off the parts, no receipt. When Trevor Donahue decided to cut ties with Smith, he followed the truck that had a load of parts he sold them for the last time to where it ended up, which was at a warehouse in Evansville. Trevor took down the license plate numbers of the cars parked behind the building. He found out by hacking the DMV that one belonged to Tom Smith. Days later, he saw a woman get in the car and was able to follow her to the address on the car's title: 1217 Burbank Road, Henderson. There was no sign of a man around.

The next morning, after the woman drove off to work, Trevor Donahue broke into her place. No doubt about it, she lived in the house. There were some men's clothes in the guest-bedroom closet, but not much else of what a man would consider essential. Most of the letters in the messy stack of papers on the desk were for Patty Emmerich, but one for Tom Smith confirmed his reservation at a conference in Lexington on investing money.

A month ago, Donahue sent a man over to the Griffin Gate Hotel in Lexington on Saturday morning to act as if he was going to sign up for the conference. When he got to the front of the line, the man smiled at the pudgy woman and asked, "Has my associate, Tom Smith, checked in yet?"

She scanned the registration list, looked up, and said, "Yes, he has."

"Could you tell me what room he's in? I've got his wallet. He left it in my car."

"Sure. Room three eighteen."

"Thanks." That was the end of Tom Smith.

It'd been four weeks since Smith had been in Baryla. Trevor had to be careful to patch up the man's trail in the eyes of Minnie Dixon and Sondra Pickering. "I'm sort of curious about him myself," Trevor said. "I hate to see you lose such a good customer."

Sondra was reading the *Cincinnati Enquirer* flopped open on the bar when she became animated over something. "Listen to this, guys. A man named Tom Smith from Ironton, Ohio, is missing, last seen a month ago at a seminar in Lexington. Our Tom Smith doesn't live in Ironton, does he?"

Donahue felt the cords in his neck tighten. Minnie said, "I don't see how he could."

"Pretty interesting coincidence, don't you think?" Sondra remarked. Trevor got up, bid the ladies adieu, and headed for his car. He hacked into the records of the hotel in Lexington when he got home, only to find there were two guests at the conference under the name Tom Smith, one from Ironton, Ohio, and the other from Henderson, Kentucky.

Trevor entered Baryla Vineyards on Friday evening with a story he had rehearsed about good ole Tom Smith.

Minnie saw him coming. "Hi, Trev. What's new?"

"Well, I did find out a little bit about your friend. He attended the same meeting in Lexington a month ago that the missing Tom Smith from Ironton did. What're the odds of two men with the same name being at the same conference? I got an address from the hotel for the other Tom Smith. He lives in Henderson. He'll turn up again soon." Trevor didn't tell her the address was where Patty Emmerich lived.

"How about that. What would you like, red or white?"

"Red." When Minnie was bringing it, in walked Tom Smith. He took his customary table in the corner. Trevor did a double take.

"Tom, where have you been? We've missed you," Minnie stated with a syrupy come-on. He didn't answer. "Shall I bring the usual?" He nodded curtly and looked in Trevor's direction. Trevor averted his eyes while taking a slug of wine.

Tom stood and approached Trevor's table after a few minutes, and asked, "Mind if I join you?"

"Be my guest."

"I've seen you alone here a few times and thought I'd try and make friends." He eased into the chair across from Donahue, glass in hand. "My name's Tom Smith."

"Trevor Donahue. Are you the fellow that owns Tom Smith Automotive, and lives with a woman by the name of Patty Emmerich at twelve seventeen Burbank Road?"

"What gave you that idea?" He seemed insulted.

"A little birdy told me." Donahue froze and gave Smith a nasty glare.

"Well, you're mistaking me for somebody else."

"Is that so? How many Tom Smiths you think there are around here? You're the only one that matters to me. A word of advice: forget you ever saw me or heard my name," Trevor said as he waved Minnie over. "I'm ready to pay up." He was angry over his man killing the wrong Tom Smith.

"Look, mister, I've got something to confess. My name's not Tom Smith. I just say it is for fun. It's really Russell Parks." He took out his wallet and flipped out a driver's license with that name on it.

"Of all the lame things to do. You could get killed playing that kind of game." Minnie appeared with the bill. He handed her two twenties. "Keep the change."

"The reason I came over was to let you know I just asked Minnie Dixon for a date. I thought you might ask Sondra out, and the four of us could catch dinner and some dancing."

"Are you kidding me?"

"Why, no," the phony Mr. Smith said in all seriousness.

Trevor got up, sauntered over to the bar, and said, "Sondra, Mister Smith over there claims he has a date with Minnie, and suggested I ask you out so the four of us could paint the town. How about it?" He flashed her an impish grin.

"I'd be delighted," she replied dramatically.

On Saturday night, after Baryla Vineyards closed at eight, the foursome entered Hometown Roots for supper. Russell Parks said, "Do any of you know how to dance?" All three nodded in the affirmative. "Uh, oh. I'm in trouble."

"Not really. I'll pick up your slack," Trevor said with confidence. Everybody ordered drinks, and while they waited for the food to be served, he said, "I'm curious, how did you ladies get in the winery business?"

Minnie replied, "It's kind of a funny story. After we graduated from U of L, we were partying with friends out on the river when a woman we'd never met came up and started talking about wanting to open a winery, and she was looking for people to run it. Sondra and I volunteered. The woman gave us a three-million-dollar budget and ten percent ownership each, and here we are."

"Are you at liberty to tell us the woman's name?"

"Sure. Patty Emmerich."

"You don't say." All of a sudden, Trevor Donahue knew he'd been set up. He looked at Parks and could tell he was in on it. "Are you talking about the Patty Emmerich that lives on Burbank Road?"

Sondra confirmed, "The very same."

Trevor thought he should cut and run, but got the stupid idea to go on the offensive. "Well, that's interesting. The real Tom Smith lives there too. How do you explain that?"

Minnie put her elbows on the table. "I don't think so. Tom Smith from Ironton, Ohio, comes over and stays there occasionally, but he's missing now. You don't happen to know what happened to him, do you?"

Russell Parks changed the subject when their meals came. The couples left the restaurant and went dancing at a swing club for an hour before Trevor took Sondra back to the winery to get her car. She reached over and gave him a long kiss and said, "Sweet dreams."

Donahue pulled into the asphalt driveway leading up to his house at midnight. He went straight to the computer to check every inch of the *Cincinnati Enquirer* from a few days ago. There wasn't anything in there about a missing Tom Smith from Ironton, Ohio. He'd been told how smart he was all his life, but for once, he felt like he was being duped by a slick bunch of rogues and scoundrels.

He lay in bed for two hours, tossing and turning, trying to make sense of the whole affair. Patty Emmerich ran Tom Smith Automotive. She owned an 80 percent stake in Baryla Vineyards. Patty Emmerich somehow knew Smith had gone missing. She'd set a trap. It seems Parks was kept away from the winery for a month, and then when he showed up again, he was introduced as Tom Smith, apparently to sell the idea he was the other Tom Smith at the conference in Lexington, which didn't hold up. Minnie Dixon knew he wasn't, and Sondra Pickering lied about seeing a blurb in the paper on the one from Ironton being missing. Therefore, the four of them were running some sort of game on him, and he couldn't figure out what. Maybe they were working up to blackmail for having Smith killed. One thing was still out of whack. Who was the other Tom Smith at the conference if it wasn't Russell Parks? Why was Parks part of the scam anyway? There was only one way to find out. He would do that in the morning if he could get any sleep for the rest of the night.

The Sunday morning fog off the river had not lifted by nine o'clock. Trevor cruised up Burbank Road in his Maserati, stopping in front of and across the street from Patty Emmerich's house. He gently tapped the door and rang the bell. She answered wearing pajamas, a robe, and slippers. Close up, she looked to be in her late thirties, rode hard and put up wet. "Ah, it's you," she said, ushering him inside. "Can I get you a cup of coffee?"

"Yes, please. Black." He followed her to the kitchen, where she poured his coffee and set it on the table next to hers. She sat in the corner against the wall. He settled in the chair beside her.

"I've got a pretty good idea why you're here." Trevor studied her guarded expression carefully as she was talking. "You want me to quit putting the squeeze on your shop."

"Among other things," he offered quietly. "I understand that Tom Smith from Ironton visits you once in a while."

"He used to, until you had him, let's say, eliminated. I can't prove it, of course." She rubbed her cheek out of habit.

"Now, why would I do that?"

"Come on, Donahue, we don't need to play games. I'm happy you did."

He was taken aback. "How so?"

Patty drifted off in her mind for a moment while drinking from her coffee cup. "Because I hated the man. You see, he was my father."

"Really. Why do you go by Patty Emmerich then?"

"That was my mother's name. I used it just to remind my father of her. She got pregnant, and he shut her out of his life. Left her, and me, to fend for ourselves. I lost my moral compass at a young age."

Trevor asked, "Is she still alive?"

"No, she died of a drug overdose when I was thirteen." Patty leaned her head back to fight off tears. "About eight years ago, he showed up and wanted me to forgive him. He said if I would, he'd give me three million dollars. I took the money, but never forgave him."

"And that's how you got in the wine business."

"Yes, and made new friends. Respectable ones."

"Minnie Dixon and Sondra Pickering," he added.

"Look, Trevor, I want to make a new start, turn my life around, and I want you to do the same." He didn't know what to say. "I'll make a deal with you. Tom Smith Automotive will go straight if you do the same and stop stealing cars."

"That's a pretty tall order," he said, stunned by her change of heart.

"You've got a really good reason to do it." Her face radiated with innocence.

"What's that?"

"You're going to marry Sondra. I've arranged it. They did most of the work, and I'm not going to hang around a hoodlum."

Trevor Donahue put his hands in his pockets and slid down in his chair. His mouth dropped open, and he shook his head. "For Sondra, I'll do it, and for you. Something dies in your soul when you go down the wrong road. I've had enough too. I guess we all need to be forgiven." He stood and urged her to stand so he could give her a hug. She grabbed him around the waist and buried her head in his shoulder. "A couple of things I don't understand. How does Russell Parks fit in the picture?"

Patty looked up at him vulnerably. "He's going to marry Minnie."

"Ah, I should have figured that out. One last question: who was the other Tom Smith at the conference?"

"Me. My mother named me Tom Smith as a dig at my father. It's on my birth certificate that way. She wanted him to be reminded of what he had done to us, and I wanted him to see that name again."

Trevor remarked, "I suppose we'll not be doing that kind of thing anymore."

# SHE WENT BY THE NAME CLAIRE VOYANCE

"These are Zener cards, ladies and gentlemen." Maurice Van Marx held them up to let the crowd see. "Yellow circles, red pluses, blue waves, black squares, and green stars. Five of each." He adroitly fanned the cards face up on the table like a magician, which, in fact, he was. He was also a cheat. "Psychologist Karl Zener designed them to conduct testing of extrasensory perception." Van Marx collected the cards, shuffled them, and placed the stack in the middle of the table. "Before I turn my back, is someone in the crowd willing to participate?"

"Yes, I will." A girl stood and stepped forward. She had dishwater blonde hair almost parted in the middle and clips above the ears to keep the hair off her face. She was wearing homespun terry cloth britches with vertical black-and-white stripes and a rope belt. The sleeves on her black sweatshirt had been cut off.

"And what is your name?"

"Claire Voyance," she said instantly.

"Come again? I thought you said clairvoyance." Maurice looked at her suspiciously.

"I did. My first name is Claire, and last name Voyance," she replied indignantly.

"Well, that's fitting, Claire. If you would, cut those cards, please." She picked them up and pulled a section out of the middle of the stack and put it on top. Maurice looked as though he intended to contest what she had done, but let it go. "Now, I'm going to face the wall. Show the top card to everyone." It was a blue wave. He guessed it correctly. The people around the table clapped. He got the next ten cards right before spinning back around to conclude the trick.

And a trick it was. A tiny camera had been mounted in the bottom of the light fixture above the table. Marked cards were being read by Maurice's father in the next room, and a coded signal was sent to a small device that vibrated in Maurice's pocket, letting him know the identity of the card. They filmed each session to prove that the so-called ESP demonstration was on the up and up, which, of course, it wasn't.

Claire crossed her arms and said, "I don't need Zeners. Do you have any unopened playing cards?"

Maurice reached under the table to pull out a pack that had cellophane on it. "You mean like this?"

"Yes. Break it open and make the deck," she demanded. He shuffled the cards seven times and set them in front of her. "Cut as many times as you like," she told him. He did so five times, and as he was cutting it a sixth, Claire's head went back, and she sneezed. "Excuse me. Okay, now I'll look away and read the cards, one at a time." She stalled for a few seconds, and then said, "Eight of diamonds." Eventually, nine cards were turned over, and Claire got them all right.

"One more time," Maurice stated.

"Jack of clubs." He looked amazed. She went back to her seat without saying another word.

"Folks, that woman is clairvoyant."

Bowling Green, Kentucky, being more than fifty miles from any big city, had all the essentials—a respectable college, serviceable hospital, and good jobs at the Corvette plant. The well-known school, Western Kentucky University, a suitcase college, had been named incorrectly. The town was actually in South-Central Kentucky, but any place that didn't fall in the Louisville-Lexington-Cincinnati triangle got branded as either eastern or western.

Beauregard "Beau" Van Marx and his wife, Maxine, liked the fact that the Corvette Museum, right off I-65, pulled in a million visitors a year, so they opened Remote View Winery ten years ago, expecting to capitalize on all that traffic.

Maxine Van Marx did the decorating when the winery was originally built. She would never have stood for phony card tricks being conducted anywhere on the grounds, especially in the room where patrons sat to drink wine when they couldn't sit outside. The winery had a cream-colored high ceiling with cherry beams. The tongue-and-groove siding was olive drab. Orange drapes were pulled away from the tall windows overlooking the grapevines. The dozen or so tables in the room were two-tops of natural wood accompanied by black wooden chairs facing Maurice's trick venue.

Beau and his son started doing their clairvoyant schtick several nights a week, between Thanksgiving and Easter, after Maxine went missing three years ago. She just disappeared one day. Not a trace of her since. Maurice missed his mother. Life went on as usual at the winery, but had begun to grow monotonous for both father and son, until Claire Voyance burst on the scene. When Beau was cleaning up the mess after the crowd filed out that evening, he pondered how Claire pulled it off. There was one not-so-rational explanation: she actually had ESP, and if she did, things could get complicated.

Beau came in the side door of the winery at nine thirty the next morning. The late February day was shaping up to be cloudy and calm, a little warmer than usual. Maurice saw him and padded out of the cellar with a big grin.

"So, did you talk to that nutty girl last night?" Beau asked.

"I did. She didn't allow much."

"Does she live around here?"

"She wouldn't say."

"Have you been able to figure out how she did it?" Beau had a serious look on his face.

"There's no good explanation. Those cards weren't marked, and I cut 'em six times."

Claire Voyance ambled into Remote View at four o'clock that afternoon wearing black slacks, heels, a gray silk blouse, a burnt-orange leather jacket, and a lot of makeup. She had mildly crimped her hair. Maurice, standing behind the wine bar, saw her and said, "Wow, you look different. Check that. You look great." Beau appeared at the door, coming in from the loading dock. Maurice introduced him to her.

Claire said, "Hey, I just stopped by to let you know that I do have ESP, just so you'll quit racking your brains."

Beau said, "Well, we know you can remote view. How about precognition and retrocognition?"

"Yeah, I have it all," she replied.

Maurice asked, "Will I still be alive in ten years?"

"Yes."

Beau stood erect, clasped his hands, and set them on the bar. "Can you tell me what happened to my wife?"

"She's dead now. That's all I'll say."

"I kind of figured that. How'd she die?"

"Killed in Mexico. Please don't ask me any more questions about her."

Maurice grabbed the hand towel and slapped it on the bar, uttering, "Oh, man. I've been hoping she'd come back one day." He looked in his father's direction while tears welled up in his eyes. "Did you know she was dead?"

"No." Just as Beau said that, two couples walked through the door laughing, intent on sampling some wine. He turned his attention to them.

Claire went to Maurice with a proposition. "Would you be free to take me to dinner in Nashville tonight?"

"I suppose. We don't have another show scheduled until Friday." He wiped the tears away with flicks of his forefingers.

"Good. I'll meet you back here at five, and we can ride together."

Beau overheard their conversation and wondered what Claire Voyance was up to.

That night, he waited in his car for Maurice and Claire to return from Nashville. She got out of Maurice's car and into her own to drive off at ten o'clock. Beau followed her to a house near the WKU campus, where she parked and disappeared on the dark front porch. He got out and snuck up to a window on the side of the house, peeked in, and saw nothing. Then he felt a tap on his shoulder. It was Claire. "Don't try this again," she scolded. "Remember, I have remote viewing, and sensed you following me here. This is not my house. Now, get lost."

"I'm just curious. You have to admit, it's not every day you meet a paranormal."

"No, that's not it. You're afraid, and I know what you're afraid of," Claire taunted.

"So, what's it going to take to keep you quiet?"

"I want to buy Remote View."

"How do I know you'll keep quiet if I sell it to you?"

"My word," she remarked sarcastically.

Beau rubbed his chin and said, "I'll think about it. Before I consider it, though, you have to prove yourself."

"What do you want to know?"

"What it is I'm hiding," he said.

"You had a secret affair with your wife's sister, and decided to kill her to keep your wife from finding out. You strangled her in bed. Your wife found out anyway and disappeared in Mexico because she was afraid you'd kill her too. Does that about sum it up?" Claire pulled a gun out of her purse that had a silencer and pointed it at him. "You run along now. Think about a fair price for the winery. It needs to be an extremely fair price."

Beau backed away toward his car, got in, and drove away. He was too stunned at the moment to think of a way out.

The details of Maxine Van Marx's death in Mexico were sketchy. She was strangled in her apartment. The body was claimed by somebody, but there was no record of the person's name. The police didn't know who killed her and refused to talk about the case. Beau Van Marx thought Claire Voyance knew who did it.

The wine made by Remote View was pedestrian at best. Maurice had lots of ideas about how to make it better and more marketable. He reached the boiling point finally and marched into his father's office. "Dad, the quality of our wine is embarrassing, and the labels look cheap. If we don't change some things around here, I'm quitting."

"Where'll we get the money to make any changes?"

"From Claire Voyance. She's gonna go to the casino with me and hit 'em for a hundred thousand or so."

"Once they find out she can read cards, they'll throw her out. She'd better hit 'em hard the first time," Beau cautioned.

"That's what we talked about when we went to dinner the other night."

"Are you two getting cozy?"

"I wish," Maurice admitted. "She'd be a good catch."

"You better find out who she is first. Claire Voyance is a fake name."

"I'm working on that now."

"Well, let me know when you get some history on her. I'm not so sure I want her lending us money."

"Dad, if we don't upgrade some things around here, I'm gone. I'm not kidding," Maurice announced with exasperation.

Beau felt Claire Voyance tightening her grip.

~ ~ ~

Claire sat at a table in a little bistro on Bowling Green's town square, waiting for Beau Van Marx to arrive. He walked in five minutes late, in a bad mood. Claire asked, "What's the matter?"

"You. I'm not going to sell. You can go to the police if you want."

"I wouldn't advise that," she warned.

"Why not?"

"Because you found where your wife was hiding in Mexico, and you went there and strangled her like you did her sister. There's an eyewitness, and all I have to do is tell the police who it is," she revealed.

"One million dollars is the price. I owe seven hundred thousand on it," he said.

"I'll give you eight hundred thousand, and you can walk away with a hundred grand."

"That's not enough," he said. She got up and headed for the door. "Wait, make it nine hundred thousand, and we've got a deal."

Claire looked over her shoulder. "I'll have the contract drawn up for that amount." She walked out. He ordered lunch for himself and brooded.

When the first of March rolled around, it snowed. Not much, but enough to cause a few car accidents. The skies had cleared, and the bitterly cold wind cut right through anybody standing outside. Beau stood inside by the window and looked at the grapevines glistening from the ice crystals and blinding sunlight. He heard a car approaching. Maurice and Claire stepped through the side door seconds later. Maurice exhaled and said, "She did it. Hit the French Lick Casino for one hundred thirty-two thousand."

"You don't say." Beau glared at Claire.

"She lent me one hundred thousand of it."

"Did Claire tell you she's buying the winery?"

"No." Maurice looked confused. "What are you going to do then, Dad?"

"Take a trip around the world." He briskly moved out of the room, grabbed his coat, climbed in his car, waited for the defroster to start working, and sped away in the direction of town.

Beau cruised down the street near the university where he had followed Claire several nights ago, found the house where she had stopped, and pulled in the driveway. The place was empty, so he knocked on the neighbor's door. "Good morning, ma'am. Do you happen to know where the people next door have gone?" She had on a blue housedress, maroon sweater, and apron with a dainty floral pattern. Her styled hair was a blueish-silver.

She chirped up in a whiny voice, "There ain't no people, just one little girl lives there. She told me she was going to visit a friend in Nashville for a month."

"Do you know her name?"

"Sure. Claudette Paprin."

He thanked her and got back in his car. He knew Claudette. She was the daughter of his wife's sister, the one he'd had the affair with…and choked to death.

Beau went into the archives of videos cataloged in the office closet at the winery. It took a while to find the one he was looking for. He played the tape several times, but it wasn't until he ran it in slow motion that he caught what made the trick. He still couldn't figure out how Claire Voyance knew that he had killed Maxine's sister, and somehow learned he had found Maxine in Mexico and gone there to strangle her. Next, he got on Facebook and befriended Claudette Paprin's childhood neighbor, asking her the name of Claudette's college roommate.

Maurice and Beau Van Marx did their card trick on Friday night as usual in front of a packed house. Claire Voyance sat quietly in the back of the room unnoticed. She had on a silver taffeta jumpsuit, wide black belt, and turquoise jewelry. She waited for Beau to appear after the crowd thinned and reached into her purse to pull out the contract for the sale of the winery. She hustled over to him, saying, "I want this back by Monday." He peered at her as though she had a foul odor.

Maurice broke his father's trance and said, "Dad, we're going to Nashville to catch a little nightlife. I'll see you tomorrow."

"Okay." He was still seething.

When his son's BMW got to the gate of Remote View, Beau ran to his car, intending to tail them. The one-hour and fifteen-minute drive to Nashville proved uneventful, and it had been easier than expected keeping contact. Maurice parked in front of The Oak Bar on 6<sup>th</sup> Street downtown. Beau eased into a spot across the way where he could see what went on inside. He saw Maurice and Claire join a girl sitting at a table. She stood to greet them, and he could tell it was Claudette Paprin. The group engaged in conversation for a few minutes, had one drink, and paid the bill.

About three miles southwest of town, Maurice Van Marx entered a six-story apartment development of white brick, orange siding, and balconies with black railings. He drove all the way to the back of the complex before he and Claire got out. Claudette Paprin, already there, exited her vehicle simultaneously. Beau stopped short, took his pistol from the glove box, and got out to pursue them. By the time he got close, they had already gone into a first-floor apartment. He tried the knob, and then knocked. Claudette Paprin opened the door and said, "Mr. Van Marx, what are you doing here?"

Claire's voice in the background overrode hers. "Let him in."

Maurice spun around to see his father standing there, holding a pistol. "You shouldn't have followed us. What, are you going to shoot us now?"

"Son, this woman is a con artist. Her real name is Barbara Ann Mullineaux. She's Claudette's college roommate. She did card tricks for money while attending WKU under the name of Claire Voyance." Beau pointed at Claire and let his arm drop. "I don't know how she learned what she knows, but she doesn't have ESP."

Claudette fired back, "I can tell you how she knows that you strangled my mother. I was in the house when you did it. I saw you. I was afraid to tell the police for fear you'd kill me next."

Claire said, "He's not going to shoot anybody until he gets the information he came for." She came toward Beau, stepping in front of the gun. "Am I right?" She crossed her arms and mocked him with the expression on her face.

He said, "What I want to know is how you found out I went to Mexico to kill Maxine. But before that, I'd like to understand why my son threw in with you on that card trick."

"Because I told him something shocking. How did you figure out the trick?"

"I got the tape out and studied it carefully. You sneezed, and everybody looked at you for a split second. That's when my son switched out the deck for one that had been arranged. You had memorized cards in the stacked deck, and could call them out. Damn clever trick, I must say."

"I learned about your little escapade from an eyewitness that saw you strangle your wife."

"Was that the person who claimed the body? The Mexican police were pretty vague about it." Beau let the arm holding the pistol go limp.

"Nobody claimed the body."

"What do you mean?"

"Maxine survived being choked by you and bribed the Mexican police to report it as a death. She told me what you did herself."

The bedroom door opened, and out came Maxine Van Marx accompanied by a police officer holding a pistol. "Put down the gun," he ordered.

Maxine, in a fit of rage, bellowed, "Yeah, you son of a bitch. I hope you rot in hell!"

Beau dropped the pistol and slumped to the floor.

# STUNG BY A WASP

## DERBY DAY LAST YEAR

Georges Courteau halted for a moment to gaze at the panorama of verdant hilltops visible through the windows on the backside of the home he and Yvonne built when Courteau Cellars started making serious money. Large raindrops were falling with a ping and thud on the hood of his Peugeot when he walked out of the house to leave for work, even though the sun shined. Yvonne left several minutes earlier to pick up the garlands that would festoon the restaurant's bar area before the Kentucky Derby went off.

The cloudburst ended by the time Georges came off the ridge and began descending the meandering hill. There had been just enough rain to float the oil on the asphalt, making it slick and treacherous. They found Courteau's flipped vehicle at the bottom of the ravine where the road ran along the edge of a sheer cliff. He was still strapped in, airbag in his face, dead as a doornail. The police thought it peculiar that he fell prey to something he would have known posed a danger, but they had no reason to suspect foul play.

## DERBY DAY THE SAME YEAR

Just after breakfast, Renea Kenworth hopped out of her green pickup truck to enter Two Wheels and a Motor, a cycle repair shop that boasted the prowess to fix anything that had, ostensibly, a motor and two wheels. The man at the counter looked up, unable to disguise his admiration. Renea had grown used to that. She smiled and said, "Hi. I've got a vintage scooter that needs some work. Would you have time to look at it?"

Alvin Raines thought, *Hell, I'd drink your dirty bathwater if you asked me to,* then said aloud, "Whatcha got."

"It's a 1955 Vespa one-fifty GS," she answered with trepidation.

"Vespa? Haven't seen one of those since I was a kid. Might be hard to get parts."

Renea was prepared for that roadblock. "I've got what you'll need."

"Well then, let's bring the thing in." He followed her out to the truck, ogling her figure on the way, stumbling on the door threshold as he crossed it. She had a list of what she wanted done and gave it to him with the necessary parts. He asked, "Is there a number I can reach you at?"

"How long will it take?"

"I'll fix it right now myself," Alvin said.

"Good. I work three to eleven. Think I can pick it up at two?"

"Sure. What kind of work do you do?" He hoped she modeled swimsuits or something of the sort.

"I'm the sommelier at Courteau Cellars."

"Imagine that. I've never been able to get in the place," he uttered with disappointment.

It took Alvin two hours to put on a new set of tires and rebuild the carburetor. Since he had a little time before her return, he pressure-washed the Vespa, put on a coat of wax, and touched up all the scratches he could find. Renea's truck fell in behind him while he was on a test drive. She honked and waved. When they parked, she yelled with exhilaration, "Will you look at that!"

"Like new. Runs great."

"I owe you big time. Why don't you come over to the restaurant this afternoon and watch the Derby? I'll find a place for you."

"We close at five. I can make it by six. Here, let me help you load this puppy." He couldn't believe his luck.

The Courteau name originated in the Languedoc region of France in the 1700s. Georges and Yvonne moved to Florence, Kentucky, eleven years ago, to open a supper club that offered the finest wine selection in North America. Florence didn't prove to be a good choice for that kind of restaurant, but the two of them slogged on for several years until success came their way. The breakthrough happened when big spenders started coming over from Cincinnati, which was just across the Ohio River, to partake in a new, pared-down menu of fine food.

Back then, Georges acted as the sommelier and was known for his legendary wine knowledge. When he died unexpectedly, Yvonne had to find the right replacement. She chose Renea Kenworth for two reasons. Renea was drop-dead gorgeous, and her credentials were impressive. She received thorough training from the Sommelier Society of America and the Court of Master Sommeliers. Both institutions rhapsodized about her tableside manner.

Alvin Raines entered the supper club to find two dozen people jammed around the TV in the bar. The main dining room had light-brown brick walls with mortar joints that hadn't been tooled. The tables—two-, four-, six-, and eight-tops—were covered with white tablecloths, and the dark wood floor absorbed the orange light emanating from the rows of sconces on the walls. He saw Renea plying her trade at a table of well-dressed men. When she looked toward the bar, Alvin raised his hand discreetly. She walked over and said, "Watch the race in here, and then I'll come get you." She hailed the bartender amidst the hubbub and said, "Tim, get Mr. Raines a glass of Cheval Blanc."

Carbon Meter, at 12 to 1 odds, rolled down the middle of the track late to wrest the drama from a three-horse battle at the rail. A man in a silver herringbone jacket jumped up with glee to high-five his retinue. Renea slipped over to the euphoric fellow and said, "Your table is ready, Mr. Hayes. Follow me." Five other men in sport coats accompanied him.

Renea placed Alvin at a two-top near the hall and wine cellar. She stopped every trip by for a little small talk, and Alvin finally asked her, "Who's the impresario holding court over there?" He pointed at Hayes.

"Willard? Oh, he's in here three or four times a week. Drops at least a thousand a night on wine, sometimes two or three."

"Let me guess, he's a big tipper," Alvin remarked.

She smiled with a twinkle in her eye. Alarm bells went off in Alvin's head, but he kept his paranoia to himself.

The menu at Courteau Cellars had been simplified to the point where the food operation was efficient and profitable. Nothing was fried, and there were only six entrees: salmon, sea bass, filet mignon, pasta Bolognese, lamb shank, and a shrimp Caesar.

The crowd thinned by nine o'clock, so Renea sat with Alvin in short stretches. She threw out some things that he figured were coming. After all, she was way out of his league. "I want you to know that I'm not looking for a relationship with anyone right now. This job is a springboard for me to one in a big city. I'll probably be here for a couple more years though."

"Sorry to hear that, but not unexpected," he said cheerfully.

"We're closed on Monday. If you've got a scooter, let's ride over to Yvonne's house in the afternoon."

"I've got several. Who is Yvonne?" he asked.

"She owns this place. Her husband died in a car crash on Derby Day last year." She got up, went into the wine cellar, grabbed a bottle of red wine, and delivered it to a table in the opposite corner of the restaurant.

When she returned, he said, "I'll be at the shop when you show up on that fine Italian machine of yours." She rubbed his shoulder and handed him the bill for dinner, without a charge for the wine in the bar. He had no idea that the Cheval Blanc she ordered for him went for $100 a glass.

Two Wheels and a Motor was on the east side of I-75 in Florence, making it easy to head southeast on the country roads that led to Independence, the little town where Yvonne Courteau lived. The weather was cloudy and cool. Alvin and Renea had on jackets, gloves, scarves, and helmets. When she saw what he was riding, she asked, "What kind of scooter is that?"

"A 1960 Zundapp Bella made in Germany."

"Nice. Mine tops out at sixty-two miles an hour. You planning on leaving me behind?"

"Only if I need to. Let's go," he said. Renea led the way.

Kentucky country roads were some of the finest in the US, not only because of the scenery, but due to the quality and flatness of the asphalt, which made riding scooters scenic and smooth. People who lived on and around the big hills marking the start of Eastern Kentucky developed little homesteads with myriad angles on making money, such as welding wheel rims, sunflowers for sale, septic tank digging, and palm reading. The green leaves of the trees were just beginning to sag and hang over the roads, causing sections of the highway to be even darker than usual on cloudy days. The two of them reached the four-way stop in twenty minutes, where the winding way up the hill to Yvonne's house began. Halfway there, Renea stopped at the cliff where Georges had gone over, and said, "This is where Mr. Courteau died."

Alvin studied the edge of the asphalt. "Somebody must have pushed him."

"Why do you say that?"

"Men take plenty of chances when they're not sure what will happen, but never when a bad outcome is certain."

"But why?" she begged.

"I kinda figured out what was going on when I saw that Willard Hayes dude at your restaurant on Saturday night, especially after you told me how much money he throws around. The man's a racketeer."

"He gives me three crisp one-hundred-dollar bills every time he comes in." Renea took off, stifling any further conversation.

The last section of road dead-ended on the gravel driveway leading to the Courteau estate. A vegetable garden was on the left and barn to the right. The hill dropped off in all directions, like a snow cone, with the house and circular driveway perched atop. Yvonne came outside when she heard the scooters approaching. The rough-hewn, gray-and-black stone two-story had dark blue shutters and a mint-green front door. She was wearing a muumuu with those same two colors. "Who's your friend," she asked.

"This is Alvin Raines, Yvonne. He spruced up this Vespa for me." She swept her right hand toward the rear wheel of her vintage Italian moped.

"Welcome. Won't you folks come in?"

Alvin stood at the windows in the family room thinking, *So this is how the other half lives...*

Yvonne set a tray of refreshments on the coffee table. Renea said, "Is everything all right? You seem troubled."

"I got a call today from Willard Hayes. He said he wants to buy Courteau Cellars. He claimed that the place was only making money because he and his friends were buying expensive wines. If I didn't sell to him, he made it clear that his crowd would spend their money elsewhere."

"Well, let 'em then," Renea stated sternly.

"His crowd are the only people that come in anymore. They hog all the reservations, and the place is getting a reputation for being a hood's convention."

"If I may ask, ma'am, do you know what Mr. Hayes does for a living?"

Renea cut in and said, "I can answer that. He's a bookie and loan shark."

Alvin pivoted to look out the windows again, and whispered, "He'd be the one, then, that killed Mr. Courteau. I'd think twice about crossing him. He'd burn the place down and destroy all that fine wine without batting an eye."

Yvonne's voice murmured, "You think he pushed my husband over that hill?"

"I'm sure of it," Alvin answered. "I recommend you check your insurance and consider selling to him. Did he mention a price?"

"Two million dollars. The wine inventory itself is worth that."

"So, he's offering you nothing for the restaurant," Renea surmised.

"Respectfully, ma'am, I would recommend that you offer to sell it to him for five million dollars, and then go to the police. If he refuses to pay, tell him you've alerted the authorities. When the Florence police check him out, they'll find out from the Cincinnati police that he's a crime boss."

"If I sell, I'll have to leave town," Yvonne reflected.

Alvin asked, "You okay with that?"

She stood and walked over next to him. "Yes."

Renea probed, "How would he have made Georges crash?"

"Probably taped a moving blanket to the right side of his car, pulled up next to him, shoved him over, and then put the blanket in the trunk and drove off. He had to make sure no paint from his car was left on Mr. Courteau's."

Renea and Alvin rode back to Alvin's shop in a somber mood. When they got there, she said, "Yvonne doesn't deserve this. She's a wonderful person."

"Look at it this way. That restaurant is in the wrong place. She would do well to get out of it."

Renea knew that Willard Hayes always came in on Wednesday night, so she invited Alvin there too. Yvonne had called Hayes earlier in the day to tell him the price. Renea seated Willard's army at the eight-top he liked the best. "Bring us two bottles of Vermentino for the table," he ordered.

While she was getting the wine, Hayes went into the bar and sat next to Raines. Raines turned to him and said, "Hi, I'm—"

"I know who you are. Alvin Raines. You own a second-rate motorcycle repair shop in town. For the life of me, I don't understand what she sees in a bumpkin like you."

"Who sees?"

"Renea."

"I don't know what you're talking about. I repaired her Vespa, and she suggested I have a glass of wine in here."

"Vespa?"

"Yeah, that's Italian for wasp."

Hayes looked back at his table and said, "I saw you with her here last Saturday night. You two are friendly. So, that'll be the last time you lie to me, right?" He got up and rejoined his cadre of syco-phants. Alvin raised his glass of wine in a salute as Hayes was going.

After the black hats finished the two bottles of wine, they cleared out without eating dinner. Hayes left two twenties on the table. It was the first time he had not given Renea a tip. Alvin watched them go, and then let Renea seat him by the wine cellar again. He ordered the lamb shank, and she brought him a spectacular wine to go with it. She said, "I guess he was demonstrating what it would be like if he took his business elsewhere."

"I'd like to take him *elsewhere*, all right." Raines manufactured a smile to diffuse his anger. "Look, we need to hire security for Mrs. Courteau, this place, and you."

"What about you?"

"I'm good."

"Why don't you stay at my place for a few nights until this thing blows over," she said. Once again, Alvin couldn't believe his luck.

"What will the neighbors say?"

On Thursday, Yvonne agreed to sell Courteau Cellars to Willard Hayes for four million dollars cash. Hayes took three suitcases of money on Friday morning and dropped them off at Yvonne's lawyer's office. When they gave him a receipt, he told them he'd sign whatever papers they prepared for the sale when they were ready. He went directly to Courteau Cellars to tell the employees that he had bought the place, and nothing was changing.

That evening, Hayes had all of his Bowers convene at the restau-rant for a celebratory dinner. "Renea, bring us the Cheval Blanc St. Emilion."

When she returned with the bottle and poured some in every-one's glasses, he got to his feet and announced, "Gentlemen, thank you for being such good friends. You are welcome in my restaurant anytime. Cheers." Hayes glanced to the left and could see Alvin Raines sitting at the bar. He said to his table guests, "Excuse me, men, for a minute. Get your orders in while I'm gone. Renea, I'll have the pasta Bolognese." He marched into the bar and stood next to Raines.

"Well, Hayes, you got what you wanted. You satisfied?" Alvin spat churlishly.

"Not yet. I'm gonna buy Mrs. Courteau's house when she leaves town. Oh, by the way, don't ever come within a thousand feet of this restaurant again. If you do, I'll have you killed. Can I see you out?"

~ ~ ~

A month later, on a Monday, Mrs. Courteau called Renea to tell her that Willard Hayes was coming to the house to talk about buying it. Alvin took the phone and said, "Ma'am, this is Mr. Raines. What time did he say he was going to arrive?"

"Four o'clock."

"I don't think you should be there when he comes. It's not safe. Go somewhere for a few hours."

"Ah, okay. Will you and Renea come for pizza at six o'clock?"

"Yes, we'll be there."

Hayes knocked on the front door at five minutes after four. No answer. He walked around back, looked in all the windows, and convinced himself that no one was there. He got in his car and started driving off. Partway down the hill, he saw someone in the middle of the road on a scooter. It was Renea Kenworth. He pulled up to her and said, "Fancy meeting you here."

"I'm going up to see Yvonne."

"Don't bother. She's not there. I told her I'd be visiting at four o'clock, but she must've misunderstood me. Why are you stopped here?"

"You ever been stung by a wasp?" She U-turned and started down the hill slowly, leaving Hayes bewildered as he followed her. Suddenly, a car with a blanket strapped on its right side pulled up next to him. The last thing Willard Hayes saw was the grimace on the face of Alvin Raines.

Renea heard the horrible noise that came next, but didn't look back. She turned around and drove back up the hill again after riding down about a half mile. When she got to the bend where Courteau's car had gone over, she saw Willard's mangled vehicle at the bottom of the ravine. He was dead. She called 911. When the police came, she reported coming up the hill to visit Mrs. Courteau and seeing the car that had run off the road.

Yvonne rolled up to the crash scene at fifteen minutes to six. The police stopped her. She told them the car belonged to Willard Hayes and that he must have been going down the hill after trying to call on her at four o'clock. She was running late and had missed him. The police let her through.

Alvin and Renea were sitting on the porch when Yvonne got to her house. The three of them shared a pizza for the next half hour while they talked of what would happen to Courteau Cellars. Alvin stood and shuffled over to the windows to look out. Now that Renea was an accessory to murder, she was afraid to leave town and had given up on her dream of moving to a big city. She was beginning to wonder if Alvin Raines could have killed Georges Courteau instead of Willard Hayes. She dismissed the thought.

# THE PERILS OF CURIOSITY

Saturday, September 28th, was shaping up weather wise to be the best it had been in years. The temperature hit sixty-three degrees by ten o'clock in the morning, and warm sunlight was an irrefutable glimpse of what shined in heaven. The soft breeze made the day perfect, but planted the seed that cold weather lay ahead in the coming days and months. Leola Sadowsky planned to spend it outdoors at her favorite winery. Maybe, for once, a dashing man with a robust intellect and degree of curiosity would appear in the tasting room, buy a bottle of wine, and ask if she were available for some stimulating conversation.

Leola knew all the wineries in Kentucky because her deceased father's business, which she now owned, made boutique wine bottles. Sales of the company were international, yet a few local wineries believed a fancy bottle could convince the buying public to fork over more money for mediocre product. Fattoria Vineyards, however, made great wine, right down the road in Paris, Kentucky, not far from her hometown of Cynthiana.

Cordell "Dell" Riddick owned Fattoria and ran it like a concentration camp. There was never any conversation on how to do things. Employees did what they were told, or clocked out for good. The reason people worked there was the incredible pay. It was twice what other wineries in the state of Kentucky were paying. Competent people who signed on expecting to make big money flourished because everything was professional, high class, and exclusive. Customers streamed to the cellar door in droves to buy Seyval Blanc and Baco Noir, the whites and reds made from the grapes the winery grew.

Dell saw Leola come in. They made eye contact, and he pointed to the table outside where she liked to sit. The side by the railroad tracks and back of the winery had huge decks full of woven-metal tables and chairs with oversized green, blue, and yellow-striped umbrellas. "Leola, nice to see your beautiful face." Riddick would court her in a nanosecond if she would only send him a little signal. She figured his paucity of intellect and curiosity kept him from determining why she wasn't showing much interest.

Fattoria's grapevines were a mile away on a hillside near one of the most famous horse farms in the area. The gambrel-style yellow clapboard tasting room between Main Street and the tracks had a glossy red door and shutters. The parking lot beyond the building was always full. Patrons jammed nearby streets during high season and converged like swarms of locusts.

"Isn't this a perfect day, Dell?" Leola said.

"Doesn't get any better. Our lunch special is grilled salmon on a Caesar's salad. Can I get you a glass of wine to go with it?" He smiled warmly.

"Sounds heavenly." The whine of an orange Ferrari with the top down distracted her as it pulled up to the stop sign. A man-about-town behind the wheel sported dark blond hair with a marcel wave. He had on a foppish, railroad-stripe gray seersucker suit, pumpkin-tone shirt, and black foulard tie.

All the tables on the patio were taken, and a line had formed outside. Dell scurried over to her and asked, "Would you do me a favor? A friend of mine just came in, and he's wanting to sit and enjoy a glass of wine in this great weather. Could he possibly join you for a few minutes until another table opens up? He's a world-class conversationalist."

"I'd be delighted. Send him over."

Dell returned in thirty seconds with Ferrari man. He was tall, thin, patrician, in his late forties. "Leola Sadowsky, this is Bruno Keen."

"Won't you have a seat?" she said. Dell backed away after Keen sat down.

"Most gracious of you, ma'am." He looked her over innocently. "I have to say that your beauty is simply a form of genius, for it needs no explanation."

She howled and said, "Gee whiz, that's the second time I've been called beautiful in the last few minutes, and the first time by Oscar Wilde."

"You kidding me? I would have bet money that nobody in Paris knew that quote. Well, you've shattered my stereotype of people in this part of the world. I've heard everybody around here drives a pickup truck and goes to basketball games."

"And nobody around here wears a seersucker suit and drives a Ferrari. Where are you from?"

"I live in Nashville. I'm a wine distributor. We deal in Super Tuscan seconds." Dell set a bottle of Tenuta San Guido Guidalberto on the table when he delivered Leola's lunch. "Ah, here is a cab-based blend we carry," Keen commented.

"Just one angstrom away from a good Sassicaia," Leola remarked.

"I must be frank, you're the first intellectual I've met in Kentucky. What a pleasant surprise." He raised his glass to her.

"Apparently, very few are left. Most become elitist and think they know better. It's hard to be humble when you're smarter than everyone else," she stated.

Bruno put his hands up. "Whoa, slow down. I need to take notes. Will there be a final exam?"

She didn't respond. Instead, she stuck out her wineglass and said, "Let me try a little of that if I may, Bruno, or shall I call you Mr. Keen?"

"Keen sounds so formal. Do I look that formal to you?"

"Why, no. You're the only man in Bourbon County wearing a tie today, and the only one in the Midwest wearing those snappy threads." She took a sip and nodded in favor of it.

"But, seriously, why are there so few intellectuals these days?" he asked.

She froze as if ready to say something profound. "Mental laziness. A lack of curiosity. Curiosity is a special talent, you know."

"I'll challenge that a wee bit. Most folks are curious about people and things, not ideas."

"Mortimer Adler and Eleanor Roosevelt?"

"Among others," Bruno said. They chatted for another half hour and polished off the bottle of red wine while Leola finished her lunch. When Bruno saw Phyllis Hoff, Fattoria's accountant, step onto the patio, he thanked Leola for indulging him in such rousing conversation and asked if she would meet him there again next Saturday for a reprise. She agreed and became curious as to why he wanted to talk to her friend Phyllis.

The Ferrari sped by several minutes later, pointed toward Lexington and presumably Nashville. While Leola watched the road, Phyllis Hoff snuck up behind her, saying, "I hope this day never ends."

"Oh, Phyllis. How's it going? I just shared a bottle of wine with your friend, Bruno Keen. What an interesting fellow."

"Yeah. He's Dell's partner. He owns half the business," Phyllis said.

"You're kidding?"

"No, but I don't think I'm supposed to share that with anybody."

"Your secret's safe with me," Leola assured her.

On Monday morning, Leola Sadowsky climbed in her car at 7:45 as she usually did and drove to Crush Bottles, Inc., the business she inherited from her father. The company employed fifteen people and made a modest profit that was used primarily to fund retirement accounts for the workers. Since the business practically ran itself, Leola got on the Internet and began snooping around to see what she could learn about Bruno Keen. After seeing a few interesting things, she went back home a few minutes later to grab what she needed for a few days on the road.

The weather had slipped from its Saturday peak, but was still pleasant enough. By noon, Leola was down the Bluegrass Parkway, approaching the I-65 South junction leading to Tennessee. When she located SuperTusc Distributing in a Nashville industrial park, she eased by the cream-colored concrete-block building and saw the Ferrari parked under a canopy in the back corner of the lot. Three red-and-gold box trucks were lined up at the loading docks, one preparing to drive away with a load. Leola turned around and coasted into a camouflaged spot across the street where she could watch the comings and goings at the business.

A white Mercedes SUV pulled in by the front door after an hour of little activity, and a short man dressed in black went in. He and Bruno came out five minutes later. They proceeded in separate cars to a smaller warehouse up the street. Leola found another good vantage point to observe what went on. The narrow overhead door rattled as it coiled up, and several cases of wine were quickly loaded into the vehicle. The man shook Bruno Keen's hand and gave him a small envelope. Leola waited for both cars to pull out before catching the Mercedes and dropping in behind it. The SUV parked at the back of the Bar T Steakhouse in Brentwood ten minutes later. She drove by and headed to the West End near Vanderbilt to check into a hotel.

Leola Sadowsky spent Tuesday, Wednesday, and part of Thursday visiting wineries in Tennessee and Kentucky. Most were small-time, rustic, just trying to make a go of it. The better ones were not as strapped for money. Many had limited marketing knowledge and a low level of business acumen, much like restauranteurs who started up based on a naïve vision of something fun to do. She arrived back in Cynthiana at suppertime, picked up a grilled chicken salad from a chain restaurant, and took it home to enjoy with a glass of wine and the music of Wes Montgomery. Before turning in for the night, she called Phyllis Hoff and asked her to meet for breakfast at Bob Evans in Georgetown the next morning at seven o'clock.

The two women slid into a corner booth at the nearly empty restaurant. Early morning sunshine flooded through the dining room window onto the face of the young waitress. She set a tank of coffee and two cups on the table.

"How long have you been working at Fattoria, Phyllis?" Leola asked.

"Seven years," she said. "How long has your father been dead?"

"Just over a year. He left me a wonderful business. Quiet, well established, with loyal people. I really enjoy meeting customers and figuring out how they operate. It's my curious nature."

"So, how does our place rate when compared to other wineries?"

"Looks to me like it's almost too good to be true." Leola baited her with the comment.

"What do you mean?" Phyllis asked. The waitress came around again and took their breakfast orders.

"From what I hear, Dell pays the help like a dictator pays military generals. I just can't figure out how he does it. I mean, does the business make that much money?"

Phyllis twisted in her seat and looked as if she had just swallowed the canary. "You know, we do sell a lot of wine, and the food service business has been pretty good."

"Phyllis, do you know what smurfing is?" Leola probed.

"No, I don't."

"It's placing dirty money in small amounts in a legitimate business or institution."

"What is dirty money?" Phyllis asked. She knew what it was, but hoped to put on a front.

"Money obtained illegally." Leola turned sideways in the booth, leaned on the wall, and put her elbow on the table. She looked directly at Phyllis and said, "Bruno Keen. He's placing money in Fattoria Vineyards, and you have to be in on it. Why?"

"I can't talk about what goes on at the business." Her hand shook as she brought the coffee cup up to her lip.

"I think you better talk to me before something bad happens. How did it start?"

Phyllis looked away as tears welled up in her eyes. "Five years ago, my husband lost his job, and we needed money. I asked Mr. Keen for a loan. He said there was a better way for me to make up his lost income."

"What did you do?"

"Keen would bring me five to ten thousand a week in cash. I would write phony invoices for wine and food sales, and then deposit the cash as payment for those invoices."

"Did he give you any money?"

"Five hundred a week for a while, but that stopped when Dell raised everybody's pay."

The waitress brought shirred eggs and a rasher of bacon for Phyllis. Leola's scrambled eggs, hash browns, and sausage looked like a lot of food. The two of them stopped talking for several minutes while they ate. Leola eventually asked, "How does Dell fit into this?"

Phyllis wiped the tears from her eyes and said, "Dell? Well, within a year, the profits went from less than one hundred thousand to nearly a half million. Suddenly, Dell decides to double everybody's pay. Ten people making fifty thousand a year are now making a hundred, including myself."

"Why did he do that?"

"Because he's kooky," Phyllis retorted.

"How?"

"He thinks by grossly overpaying employees, he'll get the best people who can increase sales and productivity, offsetting the higher payroll cost."

"Has that happened?"

"Somewhat, but not enough. The funny thing is, Dell doesn't know what Bruno is doing. If extra cash stopped coming in, Dell would have to cut everybody's pay, or go broke."

"You mean he's not in on it?"

"No."

"So, Bruno Keen's in a spot. Wonder how he's planning to get out of it?"

Phyllis replied, "My guess? He'll tell Dell the bad news and see where it goes from there."

"I'm more worried about you, Phyllis." Leola patted her hand. "We need to figure a way out of this." On the ride back to Crush Bottles, Leola rang up her attorney and asked him to find out who owned SuperTusc Distributing. He reported later that afternoon that it was a small division of a large, international beverage conglomerate.

Saturday's weather forecast called for wind and fast-moving clouds that would culminate in rain by four o'clock. The temperature was expected to drop several degrees after the precipitation stopped. A little before noon, Leola parked in Fattoria's lot next to the Ferrari. She saw Bruno Keen stationed at a table outside, up against the building to block the wind. He stood when she came near. "Not quite the glorious weather we enjoyed last weekend."

"In every life, a little rain must fall," she quoted.

"Henry Wadsworth Longfellow, I believe. How have you been?"

"Busy." She wasn't quite as friendly as last week.

"Well, set your cares aside. I brought a very good wine for us to try." They talked awhile before ordering a light lunch. The wine was better than good. Bruno finally said something unexpected when they finished eating. "Leola, I would like to buy your bottle business, if you're interested in selling."

She shot him a bankrupt look. "Why, so you can begin layering?"

"Come again?"

"You know, layering. In laundering money, you smurf it, and then layer it."

Bruno sat up in his chair, looking troubled. "You've lost me."

"Layering is the process of shifting money from place to place so it cannot be followed. You would move profits from Fattoria over to Crush by making up phony invoices for bottle sales."

"I take it you're not interested in selling. I resent the implication that I'm laundering money." His body language said it all.

"How 'bout I spell it out for you, Mr. Keen. You sell wine for cash at a discount to a restaurant. They make money selling it at the table to customers, like Bar T Steakhouse, and you keep the cash. The money is dirty, so you don't want to keep it in the mattress or deposit it, leaving a trail. That's why you place it here to begin cleaning it." The wind whipped up, adding an extra chill to the conversation.

"Your curiosity is proving to be even more stupendous than your intellect," he blurted. "Where's your proof. Ask Dell. He doesn't know anything."

"I don't have to. All I have to do is call the executives at the company that owns SuperTusc and scare people at the Bar T into ratting you out," she said ominously.

"Do you have some sort of end game in mind?" Bruno knew he was up against it.

"Yes, but tell me first why you let Dell double everybody's pay. When he did that, the laundered money evaporated."

"Because he thought the move would actually increase the profit. To quote an economist, there are too many payroll dollars chasing too few sales dollars. The real problem is that Dell doesn't understand you have to listen to people if you want the business to improve. You can't just pay them a lot of money and ignore what they have to say."

Leola responded, "If I know you, there's more to it."

"Why, of course there is. He guaranteed increased profitability with his stock as collateral. He'll turn his ownership over to me at the end of the year unless something miraculous happens."

"Ah, since you control how much dirty money goes into the business, you'll be able to squeeze him out. I've got to hand it to you. Damn clever." Leola threw her napkin on the table, stood up, and said, "Enjoy the ride back to Nashville." After getting in her car, she grabbed the phone to make a call. "Phyllis, be careful this weekend. Stay close to your husband. Keen may try to come for you to cover his tracks." Next, she dialed up Fattoria and saw Dell Riddick through the window, walking toward the phone to answer it. "Dell, Leola. I need to talk to you."

~ ~ ~

At suppertime, Leola heard the Ferrari pull into her driveway in Cynthiana. She looked out the picture window in the family room to see Bruno Keen legging his way out of his car. He rang the bell. "May I come in?" He was clearly trying to appear harmless.

"I don't know if that's such a good idea," she said.

"Look, I just want to clear this business up and get on with life."

She stepped aside and let him in.

"How are you going to do that?"

"I'm not sure yet," he said.

"Well, let me tell you how. You're going to sell me your fifty percent stake in Fattoria Vineyards for book value plus one hundred thousand dollars. I don't want you to come within fifty miles of Paris, Kentucky, ever again."

"Really? You think I'm going to roll over that easily?" Bruno pulled a pistol from a holster hidden by his sport coat. "No, you're going to take a ride with me."

"No, she's not." Dell Riddick stepped into view from the kitchen. Bruno became disoriented and startled. He squeezed the trigger in Dell's direction. Dell's response was to unload both barrels of the shotgun he was holding into Bruno's chest. The pistol flew across the room and broke the mirror over the sofa when Bruno fell to the ground.

The police determined that the shooting of Bruno Keen was a righteous killing.

Leola Sadowsky married Dell Riddick on the last day of the year when the weather couldn't have been much worse.

Such are the perils of curiosity.

# WHAT HAPPENED TO HUGO SAYRE?

The river was uninvitingly muddy and almost at flood stage after the heavy rains in March's first two weeks. Logs scudded along inexorably until they hit the gauntlet of eddies that twirled them around like high-speed clock hands.

Arlen Metcalf traipsed into The Horse Be With You, an unpretentious bistro on the banks of the swollen Ohio River in Warsaw, Kentucky, near the town of Napoleon, where he and the folks he was meeting owned different businesses. Getting to Warsaw from Napoleon took some doing because I-71, running northeast and southwest, just north of town, didn't have an on-ramp, which meant they had to follow circuitous county roads.

He found the oblong table by the window where his friends were relaxing. "What are you scoundrels doing in a respectable place like this?" he asked in jest.

Zachery "Zach" McElwee replied, "Waiting for the straw boss to show up."

"Bella, Connie," Arlen said, addressing the seated women. They smiled cheerfully.

Bella piped up, "I see you've got on one of Zach's shirts." She could tell the pattern by the collar visible under the light jacket he was wearing. "Rushing the season a bit, aren't we, Arlen?"

"The French grunt," Connie confirmed.

"It's our biggest selling wine. That's why I wore it." Napoleon Vineyards, Arlen Metcalf's winery, had been mired in obscurity until the four of them put together a website, "Party Like Napoleon," offering cookies, wine, shirts, bathing suits, and tiny clay-food replicas. They rebranded products under the names of six tropical fish: queen angel, spotted drum, jewel damsel, spotlight parrot, French grunt, and longspine squirrel.

"So, why the clandestine meeting, Arlen?" Zach asked. The waitress dropped silverware on the table and passed out the lunch menus. Bella fixed her eyes on the log that was bobbing up and down by the shoreline of the river.

"I've got something troubling to tell you. I've been getting letters in the mail accusing me of killing Hugo Sayre." The three of them acted a little dazed.

"Me too," Zach admitted.

"And me," Bella added.

Connie said, "Well, we're all getting letters. How long has it been since anyone has seen Hugo?"

"I last saw him at our Valentine's Day party five weeks ago," Zach reported. None of the others had seen him since then either.

Bella asked, "Where are the postmarks from?"

"Warsaw, which I presume is why we're here," Connie said.

"Think we can stake out the post office and catch who's sending them?" Zach asked.

"I thought so at first, but now I'm beginning to doubt it. Lots of people dash in and out of there every day." Arlen put his elbows on the table, and suggested, "Let's go over to Hugo's place and try to figure out what's going on. He lives or used to live here in Warsaw."

They enjoyed a hot lunch, laughing and carrying on, but in the backs of some of their minds, the thought of potential danger from the treachery of a letter-writing kook lingered.

Constance "Connie" Peebler was the first of the four to hire Hugo Sayre. She had a studio that purportedly produced miniature clay-polymer food knickknacks. They were becoming popular, and she had him build a website for selling them to avoid using eBay.

Zach McElwee was next to tap Hugo. His business exploded when he introduced a line of shirts and bathing suits designed with the large, colorful patterns of six tropical fish. Zach developed a Myers-Briggs type personality indicator for each of the patterns. If you bought a spotted drum Hawaiian shirt or swimsuit, you were a loner, social outcast. A longspine squirrelfish was a "little choo-choo that could," and so on. That's when Hugo Sayre had the idea of branding even more products under the quirky, tropical-fish names. Arlen Metcalf introduced wines with names and labels of the patterns. Bella Romero did the same with her cookie offerings of ginger molasses, double chocolate, oatmeal raisin, peanut butter, cranberry pistachio, and the all-time favorite, chocolate chip.

Products could be bought separately or in packages on the website. When somebody at the *Wall Street Journal* saw the site and wrote an article about it, the Party Like Napoleon movement began. Two dozen people, looking for a party idea, broke into teams of four. Each person ordered the package of their team made up of wine, clothes, cookies, and tiny clay food. The jamborees that sprang up everywhere were based on the "Who Am I?" game. The team whose players all guessed who they were won the game. The losers had to relinquish what was left of the wine and their clay foods. The whole scenario was a fad. Everyone knew it, especially the four purveyors of the Napoleonic medley.

The "gang" drove their cars over to the fourplex matching the address Sayre put on invoices for his services. The building had a river view and looked to have been built in the 1940s. Two units were up, and two down, with the high-ceilinged vestibule housing the stairs. Sayre's apartment on the first floor had a slot that allowed delivered mail to dump right onto the floor in the family room. Arlen knocked and got no response.

"Try the knob," Bella urged. He twisted it. The warped door creaked and sprang open. "Well, at least we're not going to be charged with the breaking part of breaking and entering." Bella had a perverse thought that since there wasn't any foul odor, Hugo couldn't be lying dead in there.

By all indications, Hugo Sayre was not your garden-variety nerd. Everything was organized and neatly in its place except for the pile of mail lying in a heap. The bedroom and bathroom were to the left. The kitchen and family room to the right had the river view.

Zach popped his head in the bedroom before walking over to the desk by the window. A panoply of oversized computer equipment was lined across the back of the worktable. Papers were fanned carefully like a hand of cards on the calendar blotter. He picked them up and started reading. "Oh, boy. I'm not liking the looks of this."

"What?" Connie blurted.

"These are emails about Hugo. The first one, dated the second of January, is addressed to all four of us. It says, 'You all have become rich off the rebranding and marketing consulting I provided. A final invoice is enclosed for my services in the amount of five hundred thousand. It's amazing that four shysters could accomplish such a thing. Connie is buying clay-food curios from China for pennies and selling them for dollars. Zach stole the fish-pattern shirt idea from a fellow who trademarked it and suddenly died. Arlen is buying wine in bulk totes, bottling it as his own, and Bella got the recipes for her cookies from her sister, who works in a San Ysidro bakery.' Can you believe this?" Zach appeared incredulous. The second sheet was a copy of the $500,000 invoice.

Arlen asked, "What else is there?"

"Four more emails, one from each of us." Zach handed them to Connie.

Connie read them silently and then aloud. "They're all dated Valentine's Day. The first one is from Arlen. It says, 'Tonight we can finish our business with Sayre.' The next one is from Bella that says, 'I'll bring the chloral hydrate.' Then the one from me says, 'I'll take care of his car.' Finally, Zach's reads, 'I'll take him for one last ride.'"

"Bella, check the mail and see how long he's been away," Arlen said. "Apparently, he's gone into our computer systems and seeded these emails that weren't there originally. I bet he found a way to put them in the cloud backups too."

"He's also been through our systems and learned things that we don't want anyone to know," Connie remarked.

"The oldest postmark I see here is February fifteenth."

Zach surmised, "So, the person sending the letters is letting us know that we are being framed for the murder of Hugo Sayre."

Connie replied, "He may be missing, but there's no body yet. My guess is that the letter writer has kidnapped Sayre and will release him when he gets the five hundred thousand."

"Or kill him and let us twist in the wind," Bella said.

Arlen followed with "Which means we'll get a letter demanding the money next. Connie, hang onto the emails. Let's head back to the winery." They filed out, pulled the door shut, and drove to Napoleon.

Arlen's office at Napoleon Vineyards looked like a cigar bar. A humidor covered one wall, and the red leather chairs with metal side tables painted black and blue formed a circle facing the middle of the room. The brown concrete floor had a slick, polished finish, and clumps of cigar ashes were under the tables. Connie and Bella sat in the chairs, prim and proper, while Zach leaned back and slouched to one side.

Bella spoke up. "I'm starting to believe that Hugo Sayre himself is behind this."

"Which means we need to find the guy," Connie said.

"That's not going to help. He'll just deny any involvement." Arlen rubbed his eyes and exhaled.

"I think he'll hide out until we pay him. Then he'll clear out, never to be heard from again," Zach said.

Bella weighed in: "That doesn't make any sense either. If we find Hugo, we can go to the police with the emails and put him in a bad spot. He wouldn't play it that way. Somebody else must be involved."

Arlen said, "Well, he's either gone somewhere, dead, or incommunicado. We might as well wait until we hear from our pen pal again."

March is a cruel month in Kentucky, not only because of the chilly wind and rain, but the teaser days that changed a person's mood temporarily. Bella's mood soured again the next afternoon when she turned the collar up on her raincoat while going out to the mailbox. She ripped open the envelope there to find a folded black-and-white photo of Arlen Metcalf carrying a lifeless Hugo Sayre over his shoulders out of the Valentine's Day party room. Hugo looked dead. On the back of the picture, it said, "ARLEN KILLED HUGO SAYRE. HE IS FRAMING YOU FOR IT. ASK HIM TO SHOW YOU ANY LETTERS HE GOT IN THE MAIL. HE NEVER GOT ANY. HE SENT THEM."

Bella called Connie and Zach to see if they received anything in the mail. The same picture with the note on the back came their way too. The three of them agreed to meet at Connie's studio at four o'clock. Bins of tiny clay foods were stacked to the ceiling. The middle of the room had a worktable with shipping supplies on it. Connie said, "I'm pretty sure when we left the party, Hugo and Arlen were still there talking, which means he could have killed him."

Zach added, "I just checked my emails before coming over here. The one from Arlen is gone. He is no longer copied on the three we sent. He's setting us up."

"There's one way to find out. Let's go over there and get him to produce any letters he's gotten in the mail. If he can't, I'd say he might be guilty," Bella said.

The three of them drove to the winery in separate cars. They convened as a group once again in Arlen's office. Zach made the request. "Can you show us the anonymous letters you've received in the mail?"

"Why, sure." He yanked open the desk drawer and froze for an instant. He looked up muttering, "They're not here."

Zach stood and said, "We thought so. We think you killed Sayre and are planning to frame us for it."

"That's ridiculous!"

"Your name has been stripped out of the emails, and you can't produce any letters that you got. Arlen, I've known you for a while, and have trusted you, but this doesn't look good."

"Somebody is turning us against each other."

Connie also stood and handed Arlen the picture of him and Hugo. "How do you explain this?"

"It's fake. That's how. Go to the police if you don't believe me."

Bella said, "I've got a feeling this thing isn't over." The three visitors left unceremoniously.

Five days went by before the next letter arrived. "TAKE 250 TWENTY-DOLLAR GOLD PIECES AND ARRANGE THEM IN 10 STACKS OF 25, 5 STACKS LONG AND 2 STACKS WIDE. WRAP THEM TIGHT WITH BLUE CELLOPHANE. PLACE THE PACKAGE ON HUGO SAYRE'S DESK AT 7PM ON SATURDAY NIGHT. A NOTARIZED PROOF OF PAYMENT OF THE $500,000 INVOICE WILL BE THERE FOR YOU. I THINK YOU UNDERSTAND WHY IT WOULD NOT BE PRUDENT TO TRY ANY TRICKS."

Arlen didn't receive a copy of the letter. This time the four of them met in the back office at the bakery. The aroma of cookies baking made everybody feel they could use a nap. Bella read the letter aloud and said suspiciously, "Arlen, since you can't produce a copy of this, you're still a prime suspect in my mind."

"I'm not involved, and I'm gonna prove it." He grabbed Connie's letter and glared at it.

"How do you plan to do that?" Zach asked.

"Do what the letter says so we can find out who's behind this."

"You willing to risk losing that much gold? You're nuts," Zach commented.

"It's the only way I can think of to catch the person red-handed."

"One good thing about the idea, we'll all be in the clear if somebody shows up to abscond with the loot," Connie said.

"And if nobody comes, this saga will likely continue," Bella remarked.

Arlen looked at her and said, "Bella, you're such an optimist."

"I'm not as optimistic as you are. I'm not putting up a penny to buy that gold."

Connie and Zach showed no interest in participating either.

The foursome met for an early supper on Saturday at The Horse Be With You in Warsaw. Arlen said, "Okay, here's how we're going to play it. Zach, you will enter the building fifteen minutes before me and position yourself on your stomach on the top landing of the stairs. When I come in, join me in Hugo's place so we can make sure nobody is there. We'll leave the coins and take the receipt. If anyone goes in the apartment after I leave, jump up and go in right after them. If the person is going into another apartment, call my cell so I know not to come in to back you up."

"I'm not doing that without a gun to protect myself," Zach complained.

"I have one for you in my car. Connie and Bella, just stay seated in your vehicles up the street in case, by some chance, the person gets free and tries to drive off. Follow him or her."

Connie said, "It won't be very hard to lose me."

Arlen concluded with "Do your best. We may be there for hours. I'm betting someone comes in before midnight. They'll cut into the package to make sure the coins are real. Zach, be ready to hold the person at gunpoint until I come in. Should only be a minute or two."

~ ~ ~

The Ohio River is a foreboding body of water in the dark, and the end of a day's sunshine made it more so close up. Zach took his position. He came down the steps and went into Hugo's right behind Arlen. Zach looked in all the rooms and closets to make sure the place was empty. Arlen set the block of coins on the worktable and handed the receipt to Zach. He looked at the coins one last time before they exited, closed the door, and took their positions.

At seven forty, a car pulled into the parking lot. A man who Arlen couldn't see clearly strode in the fourplex and keyed open Hugo's door even though it was unlocked. Zach popped up, took the gun from his belt, and gingerly descended the stairs. He turned the knob and stepped into the family room. There stood Hugo Sayre. "Zach? Why are you pointing a gun at me?"

"Because a lot of crazy things have been going on since you've been missing. I expected you to be holding a batch of gold in your hands."

"What gold?"

"That cellophane package behind you."

Hugo turned around and said, "What package?" The worktable had nothing on it. Arlen came in brandishing his pistol. "What in the world is going on?"

Arlen had a maniacal expression. "So, it's you blackmailing us."

"I have no idea what you're talking about. I flew to Europe the day after Valentine's for a five-week cruise through the Middle East, Greece, and Mediterranean. I'm just driving in from the Cincinnati airport after being on planes for twelve hours."

"Likely story. You tried to skin us for a half-million dollars, but we've caught you. If you clean up the computer files you messed with and give back the bundle of coins, we'll not go to the police and have you arrested."

"What bundle of coins?"

Zach rolled his neck and said, "They're gone, Arlen. I came in here six or seven seconds behind him, and he was standing right in the middle of the room. He wouldn't have had time to do anything with the package. There's no way he's got it. Something else happened to it."

"I can't believe that. Let's turn this place upside down until we find the gold." They did and found nothing. Arlen kicked the mail near his feet with the frustration of an angry bear. He pointed at Hugo and said, "Son, you owe me a half a million dollars, and I don't care how long it takes for you to pay it back, but you will pay it back." Arlen and Zach shot out of there and left the door standing open.

At six o'clock the next morning, Hugo Sayre slipped on a black jogging outfit and walked over to his worktable. He pressed a tab on the bottom of a computer tower to lift the cover. He took the gold coins out. Because he had practiced hiding a test package many times, it had only taken him four seconds to put them there last night.

The Party Like Napoleon team had a private detective confirm that Hugo Sayre was indeed on a cruise ship in Europe. The theft of the gold was now unexplainable. Arlen told Zach, Connie, and Bella that if they would each pay him $70,000, he would eat the other $290,000 loss. After all, it was a deductible business expense. They paid up and forgot about the whole affair.

～ ～ ～

On Friday after Thanksgiving, the four friends were once again in The Horse Be With You when a reporter came on the bar television with breaking news. A man's body, identified as Hugo Sayre, floated into the lock on the Ohio River near Warsaw, Kentucky. The one person at the table not stunned by the news was Arlen Metcalf.

# WIDER FRETWIRE, SLIMMER NECK, BROKEN NECK

Clyde Alderson pulled the door of the fermentation room shut with one hand while he adjusted the earmuff headset to the channel airing the Barth interview with the other. Delanie Hochberg stopped working in the grape crushing area long enough to switch the neckband radio she had on to the same frequency. They smirked simultaneously when Damon Barth was introduced.

**So, Damon, how does it feel to be a citizen of the great state of Kentucky?**

Marcella and I feel like we're finally home.

**Why did you pick the bluegrass state to retire in?**

It's the center of the universe, you know. I promised my wife that I would retire from the music business at sixty-five. Otherwise, she never would have put up with me being on the road for all those years. Now, I'm home every night, and we don't plan to leave the state again.

**Center of the universe?**

Sure. Bourbon, basketball, horse racing, Fort Knox, fried chicken, wineries, and bluegrass music, of course. Heartbeat of the universe.

**You sound like a chamber of commerce ad. Speaking of music, talk about your band.**

I'm proud the Damon Barth Band has had the same lineup for the last forty years. All of us have done well financially, and we coordinated going into retirement together. I'm very thankful for the guys. They've been a real blessing.

**Does this mean you're going to quit playing?**

Absolutely not. Marcella and I bought a beautiful winery near Wilmore. We just finished putting in an outdoor concert venue next to it. The guys in the band want to travel here for a few gigs a year to keep their hands in it. Bigger picture though, since Kentucky has millions of tourists on the bourbon trail each year, we want to offer them a concert experience with big-name bands.

**That'll be a traffic nightmare. What is the name of your winery?**

Cascina. It's on Harrodsburg Road, before you start down to the Kentucky River. We purchased it from a Napa Valley winery that built the facility ten years ago. They sent great people here to run the place, but I think it was sold to us because they wanted to concentrate on sales of their California brands.

**Let's talk music for a minute. What's your all-time favorite song?**

"People Get Ready" by Curtis Mayfield and the Impressions, from 1965.

**What's so good about it?**

It's a two-minute and thirty-second explanation of the meaning of life. Much of our music has those empty spaces between the harmonies that Mayfield used.

**I'll have to listen to it. How about the most intriguing thirty seconds of music that you can think of?**

Oh, I guess it would be the end of "Good Times Bad Times" by Led Zeppelin.

**Really? I thought you would have said something like the intro in "All Along the Watchtower" by Jimi Hendrix. Explain what's good about a Led Zeppelin tune. You know they stole damn near everything they did.**

They wrote and produced that song. Each member in the band played exactly what they wanted to within very loose confines. That's how we run our band.

**Who is your music hero?**

Artie Shaw. He was married to Lana Turner and Ava Gardner. Just kidding, I suppose it's Sinatra. Sixty years in the business, eleven hundred recorded songs, and he never mailed it in.

**Your band has recorded and produced a lot of music over the years too. I've noticed you only play one guitar. What model is it?**

Nineteen fifty-nine Gibson Les Paul Standard. I have a dozen of them. The factory in Kalamazoo had a run of spectacular guitars from 1958 to 1960.

**What makes that guitar so good?**

The dimensions of the neck, the look, the feel, and the sound.

**Is the fifty-nine version the best of them?**

Yes, they modified it to have wider fretwire and a slimmer neck.

**Gibson has reissued the guitar several times. What's different from the original?**

Just the price. A reissued sunburst model costs seven thousand dollars. The old one will set you back two hundred and seven thousand dollars. To me, they play and sound the same, but street cred is important in the music business. To stay relevant today, you need to be a contender, not a pretender.

Doesn't sound like a man who's retiring any time soon. Damon Barth, folks. He's a contender. Thanks for stopping by, and best of luck in the wine business. I'm looking forward to the first big concert you put on out there.

Always a pleasure.

Delanie Hochberg pressed the off button on her neckband when Clyde Alderson appeared next to her. He said, "Barth doesn't seem like such a bad guy."

"He bought this place too cheap. That's enough reason to hate him." She gritted her teeth and pushed past him, heading in earnest for the breakroom.

Ten years ago, Ancker Vineyards of Napa Valley shipped Delanie Hochberg and Clyde Alderson to Wilmore, Kentucky, to build Cascina Winery from scratch. Each was given a 5 percent ownership in the venture to "wet their beaks." Delanie and Clyde hung onto the idea that when the business got sold, they could retire comfortably on the proceeds of the sale. It didn't quite go that way. The winery sold for a paltry $3 million instead of the $20 million figure they had in their heads, which meant they received a check for $150,000 instead of $1,000,000.

Clyde rebutted, "Ancker didn't have to sell it for that price. They ripped us off, not Barth."

"We're going to get what we deserve, one way or another," she replied.

The workers at Cascina used nicknames for the Californian transplants behind their backs. He was affectionately referred to as "Clyde the Glide" because he always tried to smooth things over. Her sobriquet was "Del from Hell" for obvious reasons. They both lived in Wilmore on either side of a duplex, and nobody was sure if they had a thing going on or not. That was the subject of much palaver and conjecture, making the monotony of the day's work go by faster.

Cascina Winery was out by the main road. The grapevines were there too, along with the black-gravel route to the tasting room and retail shop, fronted by pink and purple hydrangea trees. On a picturesque hill, at the back of the property, sat a hundred-year-old, orange-brick, Georgian two-story where Marcella and Damon Barth lived. The house had gargantuan white columns on the porch that brought back memories of a bygone era, one when life was slower. Marcella had updated the interior by installing creature comforts, vanquishing thoughts of a simpler time, at least that's what everyone had been told. No one had ever been in the house, and Marcella had only been seen traveling in and out of the property with her husband. That, too, was the subject of much palaver and conjecture.

Delanie sat on Clyde's side of the duplex after quitting time enjoying Asian slaw and a tricked-up hamburger. She said, "Barth sure talked glowingly about his precious wife, Marcella, and we haven't even spoken to her or seen her up close. There's something fishy."

"Let's think about what else he said in that interview," Clyde suggested.

She turned and dropped one arm over the chair back. "Look up the lyrics to the Zeppelin song."

He pulled them up on his laptop, paraphrasing, "The last lines are about being alone, wanting to be at home, and pledging never to be apart again."

"Sort of fits the pattern. He made it clear that Marcella wanted him off the road."

"What caught my ear was the statement about the dozen guitars worth two and a half million."

Delanie announced, "Maybe I can get into the house and steal them." She got up and ambled to the lusterless scullery. "I'm getting tired of living in this dump. I want a fancy house with a large, beautiful kitchen, ostentatious master bath, and grand family room with a giant-screen TV."

"So do I. How you plan on stealing the guitars?"

"Need to think on it for a bit. I'll be back over in a little while." Delanie walked through the door they had installed between the two units when they rented the places. Clyde started the dishes and plopped on the couch to watch the replay of horse races at Churchill Downs. He got up in a few minutes and poured himself a small glass of bad-tasting red wine made at Cascina.

~ ~ ~

The dew of the summer morning was heavier than usual, yet the dry air signaled the possibility of what Delanie and Clyde called a California day. Damon Barth came into the tasting room and saw Clyde ruminating behind the bar. Damon said, "We're having a soft opening of the concert venue this weekend. The guys in my band will be arriving Friday afternoon. They'll be staying at my house. We'll do a little advertising, so get ready for our first big crowd."

"Sounds exciting. We'll probably run out of wine. There's not much back there," Clyde warned.

Damon gave him a cryptic stare, and replied, "I have two hundred cases of Ancker wine coming in by truck on Friday morning." Clyde's mind didn't absorb the gravity of that at first.

When the wine showed up, Clyde helped the trucker unload the cases in front of the cellar. Two big rolls of canvas with graphics also came off. They were taken over to the concert stage, and a crew of men hung them on the sidewalls. Alongside the picture of Ancker's popular brand were the words "The Damon Barth Band sponsored by Ancker Vineyards of California."

Delanie caught up with Clyde in the bottling area. "It seems that Barth and Ancker are cozier than we knew. It's beginning to look as though the tax accountants pencil-whipped us on the sale of Cascina."

"I told you Ancker took advantage of us." Clyde left her standing by the clanking bottles moving down the line. She leaned on the conveyor and looked at the floor in disgust.

The concert venue sat back from the road past rows in the grass for parking cars. A five-foot-tall concrete block wall with eight feet of see-through fencing on top encircled the seating area and stage. A box truck rumbled in midafternoon, pulling through the stage gate. Instrument checks began forty-five minutes later, and the band practiced many of their hit songs for the next hour. The setup was traditional: keyboards, drums, bass, and Barth on guitar. Four voices, reminiscent of the Eagles, testified to the professionalism of the group.

Delanie saw the band members enter the Barth house by the front door after practice time was over. Marcella hugged each one as they passed by. Fifteen minutes later, the drummer stepped into the tasting room down at the winery. Delanie did her best to appear obsequious, which did not come naturally. "How do you like it here?" she offered with the aplomb of an experienced groupie.

"Delightful. Would you be kind enough to bring me an ice-cold bottle of white wine with some gourmet cheese and crackers?"

"Sure." She poured the first glass for him, put the wine in a tub of ice, and set the cutting board of snacks off to the side. "From what I've heard, you guys have been together for many years."

"A long time." He took a sip of the wine and studied it. "Pretty good stuff."

"Mr. Barth seems nice. I haven't met his wife yet. She doesn't get out much."

"She's a special lady. I've known her for forty years," he replied.

"Do you think she likes it here?"

He goggled at Delanie suspiciously. "Oh, yeah."

The baby-blue sky on late Saturday afternoon added merriment to the atmosphere at Cascina Winery. Around two thousand people paid to see the Damon Barth Band. They drank up about a half a bottle of wine per person at airport prices. Two dozen of Barth's songs were classified as hits, so the band spent an hour and fifteen minutes grinding through twenty of them. The first encore covered three more popular songs, and the last one brought their biggest hit home.

When the band left the stage the first time, Delanie Hochberg tried the knob on the back door of the Barth house. She quietly stepped inside and listened for anything other than the muted noise of the concert. Hearing nothing, she moved up the hall to the right until she found a room full of instruments. Delanie tiptoed over to a closet on the far wall and slowly opened the door. Twelve sunburst guitars that were alike were hanging in a row on metal arms bolted to the wall. At least they used to be alike, until each one had been beaten savagely with a hammer.

A creaking sound came from down the hall. Delanie spun around to see Marcella blocking the entrance to the room. She was an attractive woman with weathered skin and light brown hair. Delanie uttered, "I'm sorry, curiosity got the best of me." Marcella said nothing. "I'll be on my way now." She waited for Marcella to say something, but all she did was step aside. The band started up again as Delanie exited the house and began loping down the hill to the winery. She wondered if Marcella would tell Damon, or let it slide.

Clyde saw Delanie come through the side door out of breath, and asked, "What's going on?"

"We can forget the guitar idea. They're all smashed up. Worthless." She picked up a towel that was next to the water cooler and wiped her forehead with it.

"So, what now?"

"It's time to talk to Damon Barth," she declared. Clyde took the towel from her and snapped it repeatedly before balling it up and throwing it at the water cooler as hard as he could. "Let's go back to the bar. We'll be slammed when the concert lets out," Delanie urged.

Damon Barth entered the winery office later in the week, and said, "You wanted to see me?"

"Thanks for coming, Mr. Barth." Delanie gave him a wan smile.

"Damon, please."

"You know, Clyde Alderson and I have been here ten years now, and the people of Kentucky still haven't accepted us. I don't think they ever will. They make fun of us."

"I'm sure you're exaggerating." Damon sat down across the desk from her, bracing for a longer conversation than he expected.

"We built this place up and only got a pittance when it was sold to you."

"I'm not aware of the arrangement you had with Ancker before we bought it."

She began to accelerate her speech. "Between what I've heard and seen, I think I've figured out what's gone on. Ancker Vineyards got the concessions and a piece of your concert business for a rock-bottom price in exchange for selling Cascina to you at a low number. That low number let Ancker take a tax loss on the sale, and short us on our payout."

"Okay. Now I see what this is about." Barth sat up in his chair and looked troubled.

Delanie stood, then sat on the front corner of the desk near him, and said, "I want you to help Clyde and me get more money from Ancker. It's only fair."

"I really don't think it's any of my affair, Delanie."

She twisted off the desk and went to stand in the corner of the room, arms crossed. "You know, Damon, you are a pretender."

"What's that supposed to mean?" He rubbed his face and leaned forward in the chair.

"You weren't playing an original fifty-nine Les Paul last weekend. It was a reissue. How would I know that? Because I saw the real dozen you own that are all busted up."

"What difference does that make?"

"I think Marcella had finally had enough of you being on the road, so she went berserk one day and smashed your precious guitars with a hammer. She told you to stop the traveling, but you wouldn't listen. And then you hit her, in the head, or she fell. She's got brain damage now and can't speak. I'm guessing your band knows what happened. They're in on the secret."

"That's an interesting story." Barth got up from his chair and put his hands in his pockets.

"Oh, there's more. You figured by moving here, you could keep Marcella cloistered, away from anybody. You're watching her to make sure she doesn't come to her senses. If she does, she'll sue you through the roof. If she doesn't, I bet you find a way to kill her. After all, you're not in the mood to give what you've earned over the years to a woman who busted up two and a half million dollars' worth of guitars."

Damon Barth went to the window and stared out with dread. "How much, exactly, did you and Clyde get when Cascina sold?"

"One hundred and fifty thousand. We were expecting a million each."

"So, if you get the rest of the money, are the two of you planning to pull out?"

"We are."

"Your tale is a fantasy, you know. I love Marcella, and she loves me."

"Well then, let's march right up to your house and hear her side of the story." Delanie sat back down at the desk.

Damon turned and looked at her. "Now I know why they call you Del from Hell." He sat again in the chair and lolled his head. "I'll have cashier's checks made out to you and Clyde."

"Eight hundred and fifty thousand?"

"Yes," he confirmed.

"When?"

"When you're loaded up and ready to drive out of here. You were right about one thing, people in Kentucky will never accept you." He stood and left the room, leaving the door open.

~ ~ ~

Less than a year later, Clyde Alderson and his wife, Delanie, opened up the Carpinteria Wine Bar they owned in Carpinteria, California, and switched on the big television above the bar. A report came on about the sudden death of Marcella Barth, wife of musician Damon Barth. She tripped and fell down the stairs in their home in Wilmore, Kentucky, and broke her neck.

Clyde lapsed into a trance. "Del, if he actually killed her, he'll be coming for us next."

She fired back, "Then I say we better kill him first." The look on her face terrified Clyde. Sweat broke out on his forehead.

# CALL HIM MITCHELL, LEADBEATER, OR PINK

Irene Ware checked each room in the tiny Italianate house one last time before pulling shut the eight-panel timber door that had been stained and lacquered with such precision that a visitor could instantly tell what kind of people lived there. If the door didn't tell the story, the off-white plaster artistry, flesh-colored enameled shutters, and manicured landscaping did. The place was flawless, much like Irene and her husband, Patrick. They were packed up and ready to be off on another bird-watching excursion, hopefully, to sight a Kirtland's warbler in Bell County, Kentucky.

Patrick asked, "Did you see the spiel on Boone's Ridge in *Bird Watcher's Digest?*" He had on his rust corduroy pants, canvas shoes, and a drab-green, long-sleeved flannel shirt. The warmer-than-usual, late October weather made him sweat. He scolded himself for not putting on a Hawaiian shirt, seersucker shorts, and flip-flops, which were now out of season.

"I've got it right here."

Irene and Patrick lived in a quiet, high-end neighborhood north of Columbus, Ohio. They usually went to Lake Erie to watch birds, but an article replete with glossy pictures steered them south for a new experience. "I'm guessing our friend Farrand saw that too," Patrick said, finishing his thought.

"If he's there while we are, I'm going to put a hex on him," Irene announced. She had on brown-and-black-thread burlap slacks and a khaki blouse that were way more stylish than her practical, frumpy hairdo.

"How do you do that?" Patrick asked.

"I don't know, wave my hand and mumble something," she replied in jest. Patrick broke into a horselaugh.

Three years ago, Edgar and Rita Carbajal caught wind of the Appalachian Wildlife Center getting cozy with the Cornell Lab of Ornithology. The upshot would be a name change to Boone's Ridge and development of a bird watcher's mecca off US Route 119 in Bell County. A million visitors a year were projected. The Carbajals snapped up a relatively flat piece of land by the Cumberland River between two hills that in most places would be called mountains, where an alluring little vineyard with overnight accommodations and restaurant could be put in across the street from the gang of birder stands in Boone's Ridge. The grapevines were simply for show. The grapes to make the wine were shipped in from California.

After a pleasant drive from Ohio, the Wares turned at the sign that read Podere Vintners and parked by the main entrance. Irene said, "I'm hungry. Let's get some supper before we check in." The late-day sun had lost its pizazz as the dry, crisp air began to cool. There were small, obscure hatchbacks and SUVs in the parking lot, signaling the presence of an army of bird-watchers who had converged on the wine hostel.

Patrick's critical eye scanned the façade before he declared, "Check this place out. Garish." The architecture was loosely Mexican Baroque, frilly and ornate. The inset tile patterns of blue and yellow had been laid in between the mud-brown horseshoe arches on the long, covered porch.

"Well, at least it's nouveau garish," Irene commented, paying little attention to his observation. She made a funny by pronouncing "garish" as if it rhymed with "riche."

The restaurant to the right felt like a miniature rotunda. The room had sixteen facets, twelve of which had windows in them with framed pictures of birds covering the wall space. The shallow dome had triangular coffered sections made of dark wood. Patrick amended his assessment of Podere, saying, "I sort of like the highfalutin feel in here. Oh look, Irene, they have osso buco, your favorite. Don't get your hopes up, though. Nobody makes it like you do." Proceeding back to their room after dinner, the quiet of the night left the Wares a little homesick, yet the possibility of putting another bird on the life list was worth the trip.

Edgar and Rita stood out front the next morning greeting customers who were loading up to go to Boone's Ridge for a day of birding. The Wares both wore something akin to a pith helmet, and they each had a daypack with a water bottle, snacks, field guide, checklist, notebook, binoculars, and digital camera packed inside. Patrick and Irene were indubitably nerds. That fact wasn't lost on Edgar as he commented, "Well now, here are bona fide bird-watchers. I hope you bring back a picture of something we don't have on the wall."

"We're after a Kirtland's warbler," Irene admitted.

Rita told her, "I hear they're coming through right now." Once the Wares passed, Edgar muffled a chuckle. He looked at Rita and rolled his eyes.

Boone's Ridge proved to be the Ritz for bird-watchers. Air-conditioned busses went to and from the trails and platforms with regularity. The pointed-top, low mountains were overgrown with a mix of deciduous trees that had turned colors for the fall, and evergreens. Plenty of birds could be spotted, but the Wares had seen them all before. They did come face-to-face with an animal not high on their list—Alex Farrand. "Patrick, a little out of your comfort zone, aren't you?"

"How so?"

"Well, it's usually Lake Erie or bust for you guys. Now you're down here trying to get a leg up on me." Farrand had a weak chin and an annoying nervous tic in his shoulder.

Irene asked, "Have you caught anything interesting today?"

"I certainly have. Let's have dinner tonight, and I'll let you take a look at what I saw."

Podere Vintners was saturated with amateur ornithologists. The chatter from the dining hall amped up the excitement. The low angle of the setting sun left only the triangular peaks of the mountains next door lit up under the orange and purple clouds that were turning gray. Patrick had his laptop and small camera perched on the table. Irene sat between her husband and Alex Farrand, who had a ridiculously large lens mounted to the front of his camera. "What'd you see today, Alex?" Patrick probed.

"Here, let me show you." He clicked onto the close-up of the bird and spun the camera around, holding it by the lens so the Wares could see the digital image. It was the Kirtland's warbler.

"Darn it, Alex. That's the bird we've been hunting. I told Patrick that if we saw you, I was going to put a hex on you, but it obviously isn't working."

Farrand cackled and said, "All's fair in love and birding. I'm going to run to the restroom. Then we can order."

Irene leaned into Patrick and whispered something to him. He nodded in the affirmative. When Farrand returned, she cautioned, "Don't get the osso buco, it's tougher'n shoe leather." After a dessert and decaf espresso, Irene said to Alex in a pleasant tone, "Hey, let's go into the tasting room and see if they have a little port wine we can sip on."

Patrick said, "I'll stay here. Bring me back something." Once they ducked through the hall out of sight, Patrick plugged a cord from his laptop into Farrand's camera and downloaded the batch of pictures.

Alex and Irene returned, holding drinks. She handed Patrick a Riedel glass of adamado and said, "They didn't have much of a selection. See if you can choke that down."

Patrick looked at the glass with disdain. "This is white wine. Wasn't there anything red?"

"Not that you'd want to drink." The crowd slowly began to dissipate. They parted company with Farrand after ten minutes of banal conversation. Back in their sleeping accommodations, Irene shared with Patrick, "Something's not right."

"What do you mean?"

"The food here is mediocre to poor, and the wine is a joke. The people that own this place aren't able to provide good service."

"Wouldn't be the first operation to have poor management," Patrick argued.

"No, I'm getting the impression they came in here with a budget, built a pretty good facility, but underestimated the working capital needs of the business. I think they're broke."

"Hence the mediocre food and wine."

"There's something else happening. They're hanging on until they find the cash to run it right."

"Where could new money be coming from?" Patrick asked. He plugged in his laptop and fired it up.

"I don't know, but I'll bet Farrand's mixed up in it somehow. Let's see what other pictures he's got besides the warbler." Patrick opened the file and clicked through it. He looked at Irene. Her expression was one of confusion. She said, "Go to Google Earth and hover over this place."

~ ~ ~

Alex Farrand sat in the office of Edgar and Rita Carbajal the next morning, sipping strong coffee. The room smelled like the breakfast buffet and wood varnish. Rita jumped up to close the door. Edgar asked, "Do you have the money?"

"I'll hand it to you once I've loaded up the merchandise," he said with confidence, breaking eye contact.

Rita asked, "Who were those people you had dinner with last night?"

Alex sat up in his seat. "The Wares? Major league fuddy-duddies. They're bird-watchers I know out of Ohio."

"What are they doing here?"

"Watching birds, I suppose."

Edgar stood, threw the monogrammed pen he was holding onto the desk, and said, "Okay, we'll meet in the woods at four o'clock. Everything will be ready. Just be sure to bring the money."

Rita eyeballed the two men, hopped up again, and left the room in a hurry.

~ ~ ~

Irene and Patrick were at the front desk, hoping for an attendant to appear. Rita Carbajal came from the back and apologized for making them wait, and then asked, "How was your stay?"

Irene looked away, trying to think how to say what she wanted to say. "Most enjoyable. We can tell you're still building the business up. Boone's Ridge is incredible."

"We hope you'll visit us again." Rita smiled as if the comments smarted a little. She understood what Irene meant.

On the way out, Irene stopped and turned to face Rita again. Irene smiled and cheerfully added, "We wish you great success."

Patrick finished loading up the car. He said, "Do you want to see if we can find that road back to the building we saw around the mountain on Google Earth?" Irene nodded yes. They rode along slowly until a break in the trees appeared. "The path looks pretty rough in there. We might get stuck if we try to drive it."

"Let's leave the car here and walk back a ways." They followed the tire ruts on foot for nearly a quarter of a mile before a wooden shack became visible in the distance. The hinges creaked when the door flew open, and Edgar Carbajal stepped out. They ducked to avoid being seen. When they saw Carbajal's truck parked past the shack, they got spooked, thinking he might be getting ready to leave, so they hustled back to their car. "I guess we won't get to find out what he's doing."

"And I'm not sure I want to know," Patrick remarked. He keyed on the car to back out onto the main road. "What would interest you for lunch, my dear?"

The Wares were just crossing the Ohio River in Cincinnati at four o'clock when Alex Farrand was chugging his extended-cab pickup truck through the field leading back to the wooden shack. He parked by the door as Edgar was coming out. Farrand bounced onto the yard and said, "Let me see him."

"Show me the money first." Farrand unlatched the narrow cab door to extract a black briefcase. He set it on the ground between them. Edgar checked to make sure the $300,000 was all there. Once satisfied, he went in the shack and came back out with a cage that had a tan canvas cover on it. He set it down next to the money and reached for the briefcase.

"Hold it." Carbajal looked up to see a pistol pointed at him. "I'm taking him and the money with me. If the buyer approves the deal, I'll make sure you get paid."

Behind Farrand, Rita was resting on the hood of his truck with a double-barrel shotgun trained on his head. She'd been lying camouflaged in the grass. "We figured you might pull a stunt like this. Now throw down the gun, get in your truck, and drive on out of here before I unload both barrels in you."

"Let me grab the cage, and I'm gone."

"No," Rita said.

"Why not?"

"Because the cage is empty," she said.

"Where is he?" Farrand was about to panic.

"We put him in the vehicle of your friends from Ohio. I'll bet they're not far from home by now. We told them to expect you later tonight. Go pick him up, and we'll be all square."

Alex Farrand was mad as hell. His tires spun angrily in the grass as he wheeled the truck around to head for Ohio. Edgar went back to the winery to get a box truck. He returned to the shack to load up everything there and replace it with cases of empty bottles to make the place look like a storage shed.

Patrick and Irene eased into the garage at their home at six o'clock. They busted down luggage, showered off, and put on fresh clothes. Patrick poured drinks for them. She liked a gin and tonic. He preferred a rye Manhattan. They stood together at the picture window in the family room to survey the condition of the landscaping in the yard and discuss their trip. Irene made up creamy coleslaw and corned beef sandwiches for their supper. When they turned on the news, a story of a truck that exploded on I-75 was being reported on. The driver, believed to be Alex Farrand, had died. Patrick looked at Irene. "Looks like your hex worked."

"How can you say something like that, Patrick?"

"I don't know. It just came into my head." He swallowed the last bite of sandwich and licked his fingers.

"We better go back to Bell County again tomorrow to find out what happened to him."

"How are we going to do that?"

"Figure out what the Carbajals have been doing before the police get to them."

This time, Patrick drove the car into the woods, back to the wooden shack. Irene went in and found the cases of empty wine bottles. She could tell they had recently been put there. She said, "We have to find where they took the stuff that was in here."

Patrick saw the yellow truck parked under a tree hanging over the parking lot at the edge of the winery property. "I wonder what's in there." He rolled his car by it, and they walked back to the rear to see if the accordion door was unlocked. It coiled noisily when Patrick pushed it upward. He helped Irene onto the bumper and up in the truck. She looked through everything while he stood guard.

Irene motioned for Patrick to help her down. She lamented, "I just found out how the Carbajals were making extra money." They closed the truck door and headed toward their car. The wind had picked up, noticeable from the soughing in the trees. It got quiet again when they slammed the car doors after getting in.

"So, what do you think you know, Irene?"

"The Carbajals built this place and ran short of cash. Alex Farrand must have recognized that on a visit here last year. He told them how they could make money, quick and easy, with the right equipment and know-how."

"And how was that?"

"Incubating eggs and hatching valuable birds."

"Is that legal?"

"No," Irene barked.

"Has something gone wrong?"

"Not really, unless you count taking Farrand for a ride and killing him."

"How'd they do that?" Patrick asked.

"My guess is that he arranged for the egg of the bird we saw in his picture file to be smuggled in here to be incubated and hatched. It would seem that Farrand paid for the bird, but was told to pick it up somewhere else."

"Where?"

"We'll have to ask Rita and Edgar that."

Patrick winced. "They might kill us too."

"Too risky. We don't have anything on them. Do you know the value of those birds? They have three different names: a Major Mitchell's, Leadbeater's, or pink cockatoo. The beautiful orange markings like the one in Farrand's pictures could bring a half a million dollars." Patrick whistled, and his eyes got big.

Rita was stunned when the Wares appeared in the lobby of Podere Vintners. "What, what are you folks doing here again?"

"We were just wondering if you happened to know where Alex Farrand was going when he met his untimely death."

Rita's lips moved, but no sound came out. Finally, she said, "Your house."

Patrick stepped closer to her. "Why our house?"

"We needed to get him out of here." Rita walked over to the window and looked out vacantly.

"You told him that we had the bird?" Irene asked.

"Yes. I think he was selling it to somebody. I'm pretty sure he would have called the buyer and told him he was picking it up from you."

Irene reflected on that. "And the buyer heard about Farrand's death, so he will eventually come to our house looking for the bird."

"That's how I see it."

Patrick asked, "Where's the bird now?"

Rita jerked a thumb over her shoulder and said, "He's back in our office. I'd like you guys to take him before the police come around. We call him Mitchell, Leadbeater, or Pink. Stay right here." She disappeared and returned momentarily with the cage and bird perched inside. Its splendor was breathtaking. The bird cast a jaundiced eye on the Wares, having never seen them before.

~ ~ ~

Two weeks later, an overnight package arrived addressed to the Carbajals. Rita opened it to find a note and cashier's check for $500,000.

*Rita and Edgar Carbajal,*

*My husband and I had the distinct pleasure of staying at your winery recently. We are making a donation to your business in the hopes that you will hire a world-class chef and enologist. When we visit Podere again, we expect the food and wine to be the best in Kentucky. Looking forward to seeing you again next fall. We wish you much success and prosperity.*

*Irene and Patrick Ware*

~ ~ ~

Patrick was sitting at his dining room table, sipping Chinese green tea when he saw something in the backyard out of the corner of his eye. He looked on the ground below the feeder, and there it was. He yelled, "Irene, bring your camera!"

She was standing in the kitchen, drying dishes. "What is it?"

"It's a Kirtland's warbler."

"A little late in the season, don't you think? Are you sure?"

"Just get the camera, please."

Rita captured the bird on film before it flew off. She remarked, "Too bad Farrand isn't still alive to witness this event. He would be angry or jealous."

Later that day, the Wares' house exploded with such force that it damaged the homes nearby. A gas leak, they said. When Edgar Carbajal read about it, a devilish grin came over his face. What he didn't know was the Wares had gone to Lake Erie that morning to watch birds.

# A PICTURE'S NOT WORTH DYING FOR

Micki Mayles sat in front of the computer retouching boudoir photos at her storefront studio in downtown Monticello when a call came in from Suella Harvey in Somerset. Suella was marrying Keith Fehlinger in eight days. She bought the "better" package out of the good, better, and best choices from Captured on Film for the salty price of $1,500, which included six hours of shooting and manipulating hundreds of pictures to be dumped on a flash drive. Micki had a reputation of catching everything that went on at a wedding. Occasionally, a picture of hers surfaced as spicy blackmail material. The "ultimate" package, with all the photos, ran a bit more money…

"How's it going, Micki? I wanted you to know that Keith's four brothers and their wives will be at the wedding, and he wants you to get a group picture of the family."

"Do any of them have children?" Micki asked without losing concentration.

"No."

"That's unusual. Wonder why?"

"Maybe they're like us. Don't want any," Suella said in an ebullient voice. "I'll be mailing your fifty percent retainer this afternoon."

"Great. Thanks. See you at the winery a week from tomorrow," Micki confirmed as she kept on making people look better than they did in real life.

Anthony "Tony" Thacker and his longtime significant other, Grace Jent, were the proud owners of Thacker Vineyard near Somerset, Kentucky. The imposing winery looked like a big barn with a low roof, clad in red-cedar siding, with a gabled stone section jutting out and down the hill to the right. The pavilion that could hold up to 150 people was to the left, up against the lush forest. A cutout in the trees led back to the sylvan wedding venue. Beyond that were rows of grapevines laden with red and green fruit. The gazebo, where sparkling wines and hors d'oeuvres were trotted out before ceremonies began, stood alongside the parking lot to hold the wandering crowd at bay. Tables and chairs were sprinkled in the yard under canvas covers for the elderly and frail to relax in.

Keith Fehlinger, the day before the wedding, sat on the railing inside the gazebo, arms splayed. He peered out at the pavilion and said, "I hope we can get through this whole affair without an incident."

"Like what?" Suella asked.

"Some sort of dustup. It's usually over money or the farm."

"Let's have the police here then."

"Oh, that'll be classy," Keith said, rolling his eyes.

"What's not classy is your dysfunctional family ruining our wedding. I won't stand for it."

"The police it is, then. I'll call and arrange for two guys to be here. I'm sorry about this, honey. I should have thought it through before inviting them."

No rehearsal dinner had been scheduled for that evening because Suella's parents passed away years ago, and she had no siblings.

The crowd was primed to roll in at four o'clock on Saturday with the wedding set for four thirty. The reception dinner would commence at five thirty. If all went well, the place would be cleared out by dark, which was a huge if. Micki Mayles expected to be there for five hours, and then back in her office to crop, sort, enhance, and catalog shots during the last hour of her six-hour gig.

Thacker Vineyard had been chosen as the wedding venue due to Suella Harvey and Grace Jent being friends. Grace had recommended Micki for the photography. Why Tony never consented to marry Grace puzzled Suella. Grace tried to hook him for years, but never could. Suella secretly wished Tony would've set his cap for her, but there was little doubt now why she wanted to marry Keith. He would be rich as hell once the Fehlingers sold the farm they inherited from their lugubrious parents, who were also dead. The five kids, all boys, were sideways with one another.

On the day of the wedding, Micki went into the gift shop to chat with Grace and Tony. "You don't get weather like this very often. I guess it's a good omen for the marriage," Micki said.

Grace got in a dig, saying, "No, it's a good omen for your pictures." She interwove her arms and leaned back on the tasting bar. Tony acted like he wasn't listening to the conversation.

People started trickling in. Micki Mayles buzzed around like a June bug, shooting everything and everybody from every angle. A few rough spots popped up between the brothers or their wives, but all in all, the Fehlingers were not disruptive. Keith corralled his kin for the ten-person photo that nine of them knew the importance of. Suella would learn about it soon enough.

The Fehlinger clan bought 3,784 acres of land in Knox County, Kentucky, after World War I. The third-generation grandson, Arno Fehlinger, father of the five boys at the wedding, inherited the property in 1989. He died seven years ago and left "the farm" as it was known to his irascible wife, Orpah. She put crazy ideas in Arno's head, but after he died, she really went loony. Orpah told each of the five boys when they turned eighteen that she was going to outlive their father, and if she did, she would disinherit any of them who had children before she croaked. For good reason, none of them had kids. The property was worth thirty million dollars.

The only farming done on the Fehlinger acreage was a half-acre plot of vegetables. The balance of the barren real estate was tied up in coal, oil, and gas contracts. Twenty-thousand-dollar checks showed up in the mail each month, and there was no telling how much of it was buried out back in glass jars. After Arno stopped breathing, Orpah did inherit the land, so she ran to the attorney's office to have the will modified. The farm was not to be sold until all five sons were married, and then it had to be liquidated. After the real estate got sold, there were final instructions for conveying the cash in the estate to the heirs.

The crowd at the marital soiree finally waned, and Keith and Suella stood at the rustic wine bar with Micki, Grace, and Tony. Micki said, "I took three hundred and eighty-seven pictures. It will take a little more than an hour to sort them, so I'm gonna run back to the office and do it now."

"Micki, would you be kind enough to email the family picture to me?" Keith asked.

"You'll have it in an hour." She waved over her shoulder as she was leaving.

"Well, honey, did everything go as well as expected?"

"Even better." Suella looked at Tony and Grace. "This place is absolutely amazing. Thank you for suggesting we have the wedding here." She turned her attention to her new husband and said, "And Keith, I'm sorry I got so upset about your family. They weren't any trouble after all."

Micki was a master at sorting, cropping, and enhancing photography, and could pound out the task in rapid-fire fashion. She plugged in the camera and set up two files, one for the flash drive and the other for extras. The first money shot came up at the sixteenth photo mark. She studied it, smiled, and dragged it into the extra file. The last two were at the end of the shoot. Micki emailed Keith's picture to him, shut down the computer, and went home.

On Monday, Keith Fehlinger personally delivered the family photo to the attorney handling his mother's will. That event triggered putting the farm up for sale, and it only took three days for an offer to be accepted. The deal closed in twenty-two days. Orpah Fehlinger's estate was now all cash, ready to be distributed. The five sons and their wives sat in the conference room with great anticipation, waiting to hear just how much of that cash would jump into their pockets.

Orpah Fehlinger hated men, including her husband and sons. The only reason she kept having children was to get a girl. When it didn't happen, she enacted Plan B. After the attorney stated who got Orpah's money and how much, the ten Fehlingers in the room looked at their spouses in disbelief. The wives of the five sons, who had not had any children, were to receive a pro rata share of the cash, one-fifth to each, which came to $5,782,403. The sons got bupkes. Orpah had secretly hoped the wives of her sons wouldn't have any children so that the Arno Fehlinger line would die out. Since the Fehlinger women got all the cash, there was a chance her dream might come true. Checks were set to be cut to the wives in sixty days.

"Suella, this is Micki Mayles calling."

"Well, hello. I guess you've heard the news?"

"That you're inheriting over five million dollars?"

"Yes!" Suella screamed.

"Some people have all the luck. Say, now that you'll have money to burn, I want to encourage you to buy the ultimate package of wedding photos from me. What you bought has most of the interesting stuff, but there are a few more shots that I promise will be of great interest to you."

"What do you mean?"

"Send me a check for a thousand dollars, and you can see for yourself."

"Who's in the pictures?"

"Your husband, of course." Micki set the hook.

Suella pondered the situation and offered her terms. "Print them out, meet me at Thacker this afternoon at one o'clock. I'll have a check with me."

Micki had two envelopes under her arm when she marched into Thacker Vineyard at twelve fifty. Tony Thacker stood at the tasting bar and greeted her heartily. "Micki, you know, if Grace ever leaves me..."

"What, Tony? You'll take up with me?" she asked. "Where is Grace, by the way?"

"She's in the back making wine," he said with a smile.

Micki slapped one envelope on the counter and said, "These photos are for sale to you for one thousand bucks. You'll want them when you're negotiating to buy her share of the business."

"What are you talking about?" he blurted.

"Pay up and take a look-see." Micki had a serious expression on her face. "You know what, your credit's good with me." She pushed the pictures close to him.

He laid the three photos out on the bar and studied them. "What the hell?" Tony glanced up at the ceiling and rubbed his scalp.

Suella breezed through the door, and Micki gathered up the photos on the bar and turned them over. "What are you two reprobates doing?" Suella asked.

"Waiting for you," Micki said. "Here." She handed over the photos. Suella pulled out a check for a thousand dollars and gave it to her.

Micki turned back to the bar, flipped over the three pictures, and spread them out for Suella to see. "These are what's in the envelope." The first picture, taken at three-forty-eight, was a shot of Grace whispering in Keith Fehlinger's ear. The second one dated eight-ten was of Keith and Grace going in the men's room together. The third photo, taken seven minutes later, was Grace coming out by herself.

"How could she do this to me?" Suella growled.

"Tell me about it," Tony muttered.

"What were they doing in there for seven minutes?"

Tony exhaled, fluttered his lips, and babbled, "Really, Suella?" He collected the photos and put them back in the envelope.

Suella walked around in a circle before saying, "Tony, you need to keep this quiet until I get my money."

"No problem. Here, Micki, I don't want these." He handed the pictures back to her.

"Little late after you've already seen them. You owe me a thousand dollars," Micki said on the way out the door.

Tony paid no attention to her, and then asked Suella, "How would you like to be in the vineyard business?"

"Depends. What all do I get with the deal?"

A week later, Grace Jent stepped into the offices of the attorney handling the Fehlinger estate. She had an appointment with him at one thirty, and he ushered her in fifteen minutes late. He seemed perturbed and disinterested in her. "What's on your mind, Miss Jent?"

"Did you handle Arno Fehlinger's will and estate when he died?"

"I'd rather not comment on that, but it is a matter of public record." Grace already knew he was the one, so she unloaded the whole story on him. He pulled a folder from the file cabinet across the room and studied its contents for five minutes. He pushed his glasses up on his nose, circled back around his desk to sit down, and said, "You'll have to get a DNA test. I'll handle the rest of the matter. Here is the lab I want you to go to." He scribbled the address on the back of his card and handed it to her.

Tony Thacker sat at a cheap glass-top table in a Chinese restaurant, waiting for Suella to arrive. The rim shots of the giant spoons on the woks in the kitchen reminded him of improvisational jazz on kettledrums. She approached the table and threw her purse on it. "Gee, Tony, you take me to such nice places."

"It's the least I can do."

"Right." She sat down and grabbed a greasy, tattered menu.

While they ate, Tony put it right out there: "So, if you leave Keith after getting your money, and I buy Grace out, can we go places together?"

"Tell me one thing, Tony. Why haven't you married Grace?"

"Because of you. I've been hoping to be successful enough to attract your attention."

"You did that a long time ago, but since Grace is a good friend, and she moved in on you first, I didn't think it was appropriate to elbow her out of the way," Suella admitted.

"Back at cha. I didn't think I should elbow her out of the way to pursue you. Before long, Grace was pushing her way into my winery business."

"You know, if Grace finds out we're teaming up, the price to buy her out will be ridiculous. Do you have a buy-sell agreement?"

"Yeah. It's a Dutchman's deal," he said.

"What's that?"

"Either party can buy or sell at any time. The price gets set when the number reaches the level where one of the parties is no longer willing or able to buy the other out at that price, so that party must sell at that number." Suella left the restaurant first and Tony followed after paying the bill.

Eight days before the checks were to be cut to the Fehlinger boys' wives, the attorney for Orpah's estate called a meeting of the family. After everyone was seated, one of the brothers asked, "Why is she here?"

"Folks, this is Grace Jent. We have new information on the Fehlinger heirs."

"We know her from Thacker Vineyard," he replied.

"There have been new developments that I need to share with you. I presided over the drafting of Arno Fehlinger's will. Arno and Orpah negotiated terms for each other's wills they both could live with. Arno's will stated that female children of his are to receive their share of one hundred percent of the value of his estate at the time of his death, provided a claim is presented before the distribution of Orpah's assets after her death. The agreement states if Arno has any female heirs, then Orpah would, upon her death, leave her estate equally to the Fehlinger boys."

"But there are no female heirs," one of the other brothers averred.

"Yes, there is. Grace Jent is the daughter of Arno Fehlinger by another woman. She submitted to a DNA test that conclusively confirms he is her father."

"So, what does that mean?"

The attorney stood and gathered his thoughts. "Grace Jent will receive approximately forty percent of the cash in your mother's account, representing the value of your father's estate at the time of his death, and the other sixty percent will be divided equally among the five sons."

Micki Mayles called Keith Fehlinger first. "I have pictures of your wife doing something that you will be interested in. For five hundred dollars, I'll sell them to you." She called Grace to give her the same offer regarding her boyfriend, Tony Thacker. They both shelled out the cash.

Keith strolled into the kitchen to confront Suella. "So, I understand you've been seeing Thacker. What's going on?"

Suella was angry. "That's rich, Keith. You're asking me about seeing Tony after you spent seven minutes in the bathroom with my friend and your half-sister, Grace, at our wedding?"

"Well, one thing's for sure, I'm glad my mother's money's coming to me instead of you."

Grace came from the winery through the tasting room's back door to have a conversation with her partner and lover, Tony Thacker. He turned toward her and could tell she was about to spring something on him. "What's up?"

"So, I understand you've been seeing my friend Suella. I want to buy you out."

"Just like that?"

"Just like that, you creep." Grace gave him an ugly smile and returned to making wine.

Later that afternoon, Tony Thacker and Suella Fehlinger were riding together in his blue pickup truck headed for Monticello. When they arrived at Captured on Film studio and parked by the front door, they checked in both directions before stepping out of the truck, each holding a single-barrel shotgun.

Micki Mayles saw them come through the door and said, "What's this about?"

Tony raised the shotgun to his eyes and pointed it at her. "Micki, you of all people understand a picture's not worth dying for."

Suella interrupted him: "Do you know how it feels to be told you will inherit nearly six million dollars, and then lose it. Thanks to you, my husband'll divorce me after getting his money, and I won't see a penny of it." Tears began rolling down her cheeks.

"He stepped out on you first," Micki replied. She began carefully watching their every move.

"No, he didn't. When they were in the bathroom together, Grace was telling him the story about Arno Fehlinger being her father."

Tony took his turn. "And since I can't afford to pay Grace what her share of the winery is worth, she's going to buy me out at ten cents on the dollar." He lowered the gun and spun toward the front door. Suella's weapon was now resting in the crook of her right arm. Smoothly, Micki slid open the desk drawer and reached for the thirty-eight revolver that was there. She shot Suella first and then Tony as he turned back toward her. Both of their shotguns boomed, missing the target.

Apparently, a camera wasn't the only thing Micki was good at shooting. She summoned an ambulance and the police.

# THE PLONK END OF THE VITIS VINIFERA CROWD

There had not been any snow in Kentucky that fall or early winter, and none was forecasted, which meant Christmas Day, falling on a Sunday that year, would not be a white one.

At six o'clock in the morning, Christmas Eve, Micah and Rachel Stutzman eased their new yellow Porsche into the darkish parking deck at the Cincinnati Airport. They had come into some money earlier in the year and used it to purchase the flamboyant sports car and a chichi condominium in North Naples, Florida, where the Midwest nouveau riche hung out. The plan was to spend until the 29th flitting from party to party, chatting with people who sported pearly white teeth, designer clothes, and gaudy jewelry. The two-hour flight to Ft. Myers was leaving on time at 7:30. As they walked briskly toward the main terminal, Micah peeked back at his vehicle with satisfaction, and Rachel raised the fur collar on her suede coat to fight off the biting breeze.

Dale Metzger loitered outside flight security and watched the Stutzmans pass through without any trouble. He grinned weakly and headed for the terminal exit. His brother Max stood by the bag-claim door, falling in behind as they got outside. The Metzger brothers had carefully swept the garage and baggage area to confirm there weren't any cameras to record their movements. Security cameras were positioned all over the main terminal, but that couldn't be helped. They found the yellow Porsche and checked to make sure nobody was nearby.

Dale stood by the driver's door and pressed the fob to open the car while Max removed screws that affixed the Kentucky license plate. He swapped the plate with the one he had tucked in his jacket and screwed the decoy on. Dale removed the garage door opener from the visor over the steering wheel. They relocked the Porsche and hustled seven rows over to the Ford Taurus with the California plates. Dale paid the parking, and the brothers drove away inconspicuously. After they merged south on I-75, Max spotted the IHOP in Florence, Kentucky, so they stopped to fill up on eggs, bacon, pancakes, and black coffee.

~ ~ ~

"What can I get you, sir?" Brianna Decker asked the fellow rubbing his hands together to warm them as he sidled up to the blue marble bar inside Vitis Vinifera. He was a grandee if there ever was one. The silver double-breasted suit he wore had been tailored to fit his rangy frame. He had an aquiline nose, thick eyebrows, and nary a hair showed on his pate or chest under an unbuttoned shirt of black-and-white thread. If the watch he wore wasn't a real Rolex, it was a good copy.

"I understand this place has the biggest wine selection in the state of Kentucky. What vin jaune do you have?" he asked.

"I've never heard of it," Brianna said. She gave him her full attention.

"My dear, vin jaune is French for yellow wine. It's very dry and very delicious. Okay then, what retsinas do you carry?"

"Nope. None."

"Come now, this place is supposed to have a complete offering," he responded imperiously.

"What is retsina?" Brianna propped her forearms on the bar top and moved her face closer to his. She shifted her eyes from one of his to the other, back and forth.

"Wine of the gods. Greek. Dry. Delicious." He began carefully examining her features. She had a cartilaginous nose, frizzy hairline, and shoulder-length black hair that had not been fussed with. Her eyes were big, baby blue, and wide-set. "Okay, how about orange wine?"

"What we have here is red, brown, or white. Surely you can think of something in those colors."

"Orange wine is both red and white. Made like red wine, but with white grapes." He exhaled in frustration. "Okay then, just give me the best noble rot you've got."

"Noble rot?"

"It's a sweet dessert wine. I give up. Bring me a glass of the most expensive thing you have."

"Domaine de la Romanée-Conti. Three hundred bucks a glass," she warned.

"Ah, DRC, now we're getting somewhere. Don't skimp on the pour," he demanded.

When she brought the wine, she asked, "Who are you, and why are you here by yourself the day before Christmas?"

"Sampson LeGrand, distinguished oenophile from California, here because I was told the bar is going to close for several days. I've been commissioned to write a column on this establishment before the end of the year, and didn't want to cram it all in after the holiday."

"My name's Brianna Decker, distinguished bartender, and I'm not married. We close at eight. What say you come over to my place a little later for some holiday cheer?" She handed him her address. He grinned and jammed it in the front pocket of his suit coat. Sampson settled the bill when his glass was empty, and Brianna watched him climb into a yellow Porsche parked out front.

~ ~ ~

After dark, on Christmas Eve, the Metzger brothers drove into the Stutzmans' garage, dropping the overhead door behind them. They quickly stepped inside to disarm the alarm. Dale flipped on a flashlight and led the way to the master bedroom, where a big black safe was tucked in the closet. He punched the combination onto the electronic keypad to unlock the heavy door. Max said, "You see a passport in there?"

Dale replied, "Yeah, along with the gold coins." They pulled the bottle of DRC they brought with them out of the cloth bag it was in and filled the bag with the coins. Max laid the bottle of wine that had the note taped to it on the top shelf of the safe and slipped Micah Stutzman's passport into his jacket pocket. They set the alarm again before rolling quietly back out to the main road. The temperature read thirty-seven degrees on the Taurus dashboard. "I've had about enough of this cold weather," Dale lamented.

Vitis Vinifera was owned by a boutique hotel chain based in Canada. It opened three years ago next to the Ruth's Chris Steak House in Louisville. Micah Stutzman, a savvy wine buyer, became its manager at the beginning of the year. The owner of the wine bar had advised him to keep the inventory at two million. When he got a chance to buy the batch of DRC, Domaine de la Romanée-Conti, for a hundred thousand, he bought it personally and sold it to Vitis Vinifera for four hundred thousand. It was worth six hundred, so, no harm, no foul. He'd done that sort of thing on several transactions, hence the car, condo, and coins. Some deals seemed too good to be true, so he made sure the merchandise was authentic before he bought it. The inventory evaluation done by corporate just before Micah and Rachel took their vacation determined the wine in stock was worth two hundred thousand more than it had cost.

Rachel pushed away from the glass table when she finished the midafternoon Christmas meal, and stated, "That was fantastic." The unbelievable Naples weather didn't make it feel like the holiday season. She wiped her lips with her napkin and deftly reapplied lipstick. "Micah, I want to run over and see my mother in Miami tomorrow. I'll leave early and try to get back by eight o'clock."

He looked up at her and responded, "Okay, I'll spend the day at the beach and pick out a good wine spot for dinner."

~ ~ ~

Christmas night, Max Metzger boarded a flight to Punta Gorda, a small airport fifty miles north of Naples, to start in motion the elaborate plan. When he got there, he moved over to the ticket counter of the airline and said, "I'd like to buy a trip to Cincinnati and back for tomorrow." He handed her Micah Stutzman's passport. She glanced at his face and compared it to the picture. He asked, "What are the flight times?"

The woman processing the ticket said robotically, "Leaves at eight forty-five in the morning and flies out of Cincinnati at four ten tomorrow afternoon."

Rachel left for Miami the day after Christmas at six forty in the morning. Max emerged from the baggage claim area in Cincinnati at ten after eleven. Dale was waiting at the curb in the Taurus at the end of the line of traffic. "Everything go as planned?"

"Like clockwork. Why would anybody want to live in this freezing cold?" He shivered comically and blew warm air into his balled hands.

They drove to the hotel in Louisville in a little more than an hour, pulling in next to the yellow Porsche upon arrival. Max swapped license plates, climbed in, fired the machine up, and took off. Dale followed at a distance.

At twelve forty-five, Max turned into Vitis Vinifera and wheeled the car around back. He parked at the dock area, used a key to enter the premises and code to defeat the alarm. It took him ten minutes to load the eight cases in the Porsche, four in the passenger seat and floor, and four in the front trunk. He reset the alarm and drove out at one o'clock sharp.

~ ~ ~

Sampson LeGrand, sitting casually in the restaurant of the hotel he was staying in, stared across the lunch table at Brianna Decker. She was a marvelous woman as far as he was concerned. She asked, "Where's your yellow car?"

"Oh, I took it to the rental agency to have a tire looked at," he lied. "I'll get it back tonight."

"Are you going to take me out to dinner then?"

LeGrand sat up in his seat and said, "I'll come for you at, say, seven?"

~ ~ ~

Time was running tight to load the stolen goods and get the cars back where they belonged. Max hit the I-65 Bridge at one fifteen. Dale took the downtown bridge into Indiana at about the same time. They met on a side street in New Albany to put the wine in the Ford next to the bag of gold coins. It was one forty when Max sped over the I-65 Bridge going south. Dale caught up with him again in the parking lot of LeGrand's hotel, east of Louisville. He swapped the plates on the Porsche one more time, and then threw the keys under the floor mat and jumped back in the Taurus with Dale.

It was three twenty when the Metzger brothers pulled into the Cincinnati parking deck. Dale let Max out at Micah's car, and he had the license plate changed and the garage door opener back over the steering wheel in three minutes. The last thing Max did was switch parking tickets, placing the one they just received in the Porsche for the one the Stutzmans were given the day they left. He handed it to Dale when he drove by. Max took off for the terminal at a dead run. He cleared security and made it to the plane leaving for Florida with five minutes to spare.

Max stepped out of the terminal in Punta Gorda at six forty. He saw Rachel Stutzman waving at him from a car parked across the street. He walked over and handed her Micah's passport, key fob for the Porsche, and a piece of paper with writing on it. She said, "Boy, you do look like my husband."

Max ignored that and told her, "There's the address where you can pick up your cash. The gold coins are worth three hundred and forty thousand. You'll have to show identification and sign a receipt for the money."

"Gladly," she replied, looking over her shoulder to back out of the parking spot.

The warm breeze tempted Max to delay his flight back to Cincinnati, but he thought better of it. Rachel Stutzman entered her condominium complex in North Naples at ten before eight.

~ ~ ~

At that moment, Brianna Decker sat with Sampson LeGrand at Ruth's Chris Steak House next to Vitis Vinifera. She knew the bar manager there whose day job was in the parts department at a local Ford dealership. She always got royal treatment when she came in. "Why are you driving a yellow Porsche?" she asked Sampson.

"I usually rent one in the city I visit. Have to keep up appearances, you know." He didn't care to belabor the subject.

"Micah Stutzman, my boss, has a car just like yours. They ain't cheap," she said.

"Nothing worth having in this world is cheap, my dear." He swallowed the last of his tawny port and called for the bill.

On the morning of December 27th, the Metzger brothers stood in LeGrand's hotel lobby, waiting for Sampson to come down from his room. When he did, the three of them went into the parking lot to inspect the cargo in the trunk of the Taurus. Dale opened one of the wine cases and presented a bottle for inspection. "Yes, what a beautiful sight," Max said. Max loosened the bag with the coins in it. He took one of the twenty-dollar gold pieces out and cupped it in the palm of his hand. "You counted them, right? Two hundred?"

"We did," said the Metzgers in unison. Max put the coin back in the bag and shut the trunk.

"Okay," Sampson said. "Here's fifty thousand in cash for each of you. I presume you fellows can Uber wherever you care to go. It's been nice knowing you." The brothers turned their backs and scooted away from the car without another word. LeGrand took a pair of gloves from his pocket and put them on as he got into the yellow Porsche parked four cars down from the Taurus.

Brianna saw Sampson pull up in front of her place. She locked her apartment and went out to meet him. They drove to Panera Bread for breakfast. "Well, Brianna, I finished the article on your wine bar and sent it to the magazine to be published in the February edition."

"You were kind to us, I presume?"

"After the good time you've shown me, I wouldn't think of writing a bad word about the place. I'll be in Lexington most of today visiting wine bars. I'm returning to California in the morning, and I hope you'll come visit me sometime."

"Why, of course," she replied suggestively. "I'd love to." They hugged each other warmly when he dropped her off at home. Brianna wasn't sure what didn't exactly add up, but she intended to find out.

164

LeGrand returned the Porsche to the rental agency across the street from his hotel on Tuesday night and began the two-day drive to California in the Ford Taurus on Wednesday morning, the 28th of December.

~ ~ ~

Micah and Rachel Stutzman landed at the Cincinnati airport late on the morning of the 29th. The low-hanging gray clouds and unrelenting frigid breeze crushed the euphoria they felt moments ago. When they went to pay the parking fee, Micah commented, "That doesn't seem like enough. We've been gone a little more than five days, and they only charged me for three."

"That's a deal," she said.

When they walked into their house midafternoon, Rachel went straight for the safe and put her jewelry in it. She also put Micah's passport and the Porsche key fob back. "Micah, what's going on? There's a wine bottle on the top shelf, and all of the gold coins are gone."

He came in, surveyed the situation in a panic, and said, "Someone has broken into the safe." He clutched the wine bottle by the neck and saw the note on the front of it.

*Mr. Stutzman,*

*Thank you for making the final payment for the DRC you bought in gold coins. We appreciate it. I understand you have taken the most expensive bottles in the lot and sold them to someone in southern Indiana. I hope your wine bar made a good profit on them. We'll contact you when we have more expensive wines available for purchase.*

*Robert Parker*

Micah ran to the garage, got in his Porsche, and drove off in a hurry to Vitis Vinifera. The place would be reopening in two hours after being closed for five days.

Brianna Decker was standing behind the bar when Micah rushed in. "Whoa, cowboy. What's the hurry?"

Micah had a grim look on his face. "Is any of the wine missing?"

"Well, as a matter of fact, eight cases of plonk are gone."

"Which plonk?" he asked.

"You know, the stuff you hauled out of here on Monday. Eight cases worth a thousand dollars total," she said, smiling.

"What are you talking about?" He was completely confused at that point.

"Well, that's not really what happened. What really happened was a man impersonating you, driving a Porsche like yours, stole the most expensive Conti we have worth a half million."

"How do you know that?"

"It's on the security tape, and I'll bet the thief went across the I-65 Bridge to have your tags photographed."

"Oh, no," he wailed.

Brianna put her hand up in front of her face, palm facing Micah. "Not to worry, I stole it back."

"What? How did you do that?"

"I figured out where it was and switched it out for the plonk."

"Where was it?" he asked.

"In the trunk of a Ford Taurus in a hotel parking lot. It's a long story. I'll tell you later."

"How did you get in the trunk?"

"Marcus, who runs the bar next door at the steak house, works at a Ford dealership. You know, you ought to be happy that I like men, and they like me."

"So, what did he do?" Micah was beginning to feel this story might have a happy ending.

"I took the vehicle identification number to him, and he looked in the database for the keyless entry code and numbers to push to open the trunk." She began wiping down the bar with a wet towel.

"Brianna, you've saved my life, or at least my financial life." He stuck his arms out to the side and said, "I love you."

"One more thing you should consider. Your rotten wife is in on it. He couldn't have done the job without her help. I'm sure he paid her handsomely."

"Who is he?"

"Sampson LeGrand. He lives in Napa Valley."

Stutzman began connecting the dots. "Three hundred forty thousand in gold coins are missing from my safe at home. That's how he must have paid her."

Brianna stopped wiping the counter and looked at him. "If you really love me, I might be able to find those gold coins for you. I mean, if you're willing to dump your wife and take up with me."

"In a heartbeat," he said like a chorus of amen in church.

~ ~ ~

Sampson LeGrand pulled into the long driveway of his palatial estate in Napa Valley just before suppertime. He eagerly opened the trunk, took out one of the wine bottles, looked at it in utter disbelief, screamed, and threw it as far as he could across the yard. He retrieved his phone and frantically made a call. "Rachel, I want my money back!" he yelled.

LeGrand hadn't figured out yet that the gold coins had been swapped out too.

# FISHING BY MISADVENTURE

Quentin Lemaster could thread the needle with his rickety, two-wheel trailer by merely looking in the mirrors. He eased down the slippery ramp until the fishing boat began floating freely, still tethered to the winch. He stepped delicately on the slimy concrete, climbed aboard, pulled the motor rope until the undersized outboard engine began to whine, and then unhooked the craft to drive it around to the loading dock. Quentin parked his fifteen-year-old Ford Explorer among the other rigs as he had done lots of times since his wife died five years ago. If it wasn't windy, rainy, or cold, he would put in virtually every Friday night at the Paragon ramp, east of the main section of Cave Run Lake, to do some serious fishing. Often, he stayed out overnight, and was leaning that way this evening because of the pleasant weather forecast.

Lemaster cruised under the Highway 519 Bridge and worked his way east toward Craney. When he got into shallow water, he started floating with the current, back in the direction of Paragon, dragging a half-dozen lures and baited hooks at different depths. He would anchor on the shore regularly for a sandwich break, quick nap, or to fish a hot spot. At midnight, after catching three bass, Quentin stretched out for a few winks. He awoke refreshed, four hours later, and dropped the lines back in the water. By seven o'clock, the misty haze showed signs of lifting as he drifted under the bridge. He heard a vehicle come to a stop overhead. The surreal event that happened next startled and confused him; a girl with a concrete block hooked to her right ankle screamed, plunged into the water, and disappeared under the surface.

Quentin threw the anchor line out and scrambled over to his tackle box. He grabbed the pair of pliers with wire cutters that he kept in there for removing fishhooks and crimping sinkers. Over the side he went where she had gone under. He swam down, abruptly bumping heads with her. It took what seemed like forever to cut the bare wire looped through the block, releasing her to float to safety. Both of them coughed and gasped for air as they swam to the apron of concrete at the foot of the bridge. Quentin helped her into the boat, asking, "Who did this to you?"

"Friends of The Light." She tossed her hair back and wrapped it in the towel he handed her. The soggy, wheat-colored cotton dress that she wore clung to her torso, and her legs and feet were bare. She was beautiful, roughly the same age as his daughter, who had been missing for seven years now.

"The Light?"

"Yes, a messenger from the Supreme Being." She pulled the towel off her hair to dry her arms and legs. There was an angry cut above the ankle where the wire had been. Watered-down blood trickled onto her foot.

Quentin said, "Here, you better let me wrap that up." Not being the least bit shy, she stuck her leg out to him. "What's your name?"

"Serenity."

"Well, Serenity, where would you like me to take you?"

"To your house, if your wife doesn't mind."

"I'm not married," he replied. Serenity worked her way to the back of the boat to hug him, nearly flipping them both into the water again.

On the trip to Wrigley, where Quentin Lemaster lived in the mansard house he built behind the post office when his daughter, Carrie, was in the eleventh grade, Serenity said nothing. Carrie had disappeared the day she was to graduate from high school. His wife died from cancer two years later. To keep busy, Quentin did taxes now for poor people who lived in the mountains, as well as fished Cave Run Lake, merely a twenty-minute ride up the road, when he had the time, and he had plenty of it. He didn't have to work much because of the million-dollar life insurance policy that paid off on his wife. He bought AT&T stock with some of the money and lived comfortably off the dividends.

Quentin opened the garage doors to park the fishing boat and SUV. He told Serenity to go in the house and make herself at home. A few minutes later, after a shower, she appeared wearing one of his T-shirts and a pair of his short pants. She had re-dressed the cut on her ankle with gauze and tape that she found under the bathroom sink. He looked at her inquisitively before saying, "I should go to Walmart and get you something to wear."

"Would you? Size four clothes, size seven shoes." She smiled at him and continued, "And some underwear and socks." Serenity came over and gave him another affectionate hug. He stroked her back as a pall of sorrow came over him again.

Serenity sat on the sofa with her new clothes on and asked, "What's your name?"

"Quentin Lemaster." He sat down next to her in a side chair, holding a coffee cup. "Would you like something to drink?"

"No, thanks." She leaned forward, resting her arms on her thighs.

"Just so you know, my daughter disappeared seven years ago and my wife died two years after that. You look to be about the same age as Carrie, and you remind me of her. She just up and went one day."

"I can tell you're sad," she calmly said.

"Serenity, you should tell me why someone tried to drown you." Quentin leaned in close to her face.

171

"The police were on the way to the compound early this morning. Daydream somehow got to a phone and called them to report she was being held there against her will."

"Daydream? Who is she?"

"The Light's chosen one."

"So, why try to drown you?" Quentin asked.

"Because they had to get rid of me in a hurry," she replied. "I was Daydream's friend, and they were afraid I'd tell the police the truth."

"Who is they?"

"I told you, Friends of The Light." She seemed perturbed.

"What do you mean, friends?"

"The council that runs the commune. There are six of them."

"Are they women or men?"

"The Light doesn't recognize sex. Everyone is the same in its eyes."

"It? Is The Light male or female? You're certainly a woman."

"I'm not really sure." She got up and walked across the living room. "That's enough questions for a while. Would you take me for a ride? I've not been off the commune since I was assigned there on my eighteenth birthday."

"One more question. How long ago was that?"

"Seven years."

The dry air smelled of wild onions and freshly mown grass. Intermittent rain through the early part of summer had kept the flora a vibrant shade of green. Quentin let the wind whistle through the open windows as he and Serenity sped toward Daniel Boone National Forest. "Is the commune near where they dropped you in the lake?" he asked.

"I don't know. I saw the address on the mail that came in, 9400 Highway 36, Frenchburg." Quentin put the address in his phone and hit the "go" button. "Please don't go there. I'm worried they'll keep trying to kill me."

"I just want to drive by the entrance to see where it is. No need to be afraid. I won't let anybody hurt you ever again." He gave her a reassuring look.

When they approached the location, Serenity straightened in her seat and said, "There's how to get in. The house is in the woods a long way back from the highway. It has a tall fence around it with metal gates that are kept locked." There were also gates right off the road, cut into the hill, standing open.

Quentin pointed out all of the sights for the next hour, returning to his house after making a big loop through the forest. When they went back in the living room to sit, Serenity said, "I'm tired. Would you mind if I took a nap?"

"Please do. You can have the bedroom down the hall to the right."

Serenity, her hair combed and pulled back in a ponytail, reappeared late in the afternoon. She pronounced, "I'm hungry. Can we get something to eat?"

"Sure. Will you eat pizza?"

"That would be great. I haven't had one in years." She walked over to him and rubbed his arm.

"Let's go." He called the order in to Giovanni's in West Liberty.

On the way back to Quentin's house with the pizza, Serenity asked, "Is that a picture of Carrie next to the bed in the room where I took a nap?"

"Uh-huh."

"I know her. She was assigned to the commune the same time as me, seven years ago. She is called Tranquility. I have spoken to her a few times."

Quentin pulled into the driveway at his house, turned off the vehicle, put his head back, looked up, and said nothing. Finally, he muttered, "I can't believe she's been this close all these years." He turned to Serenity and asked, "Is she all right? I mean, like, mentally and physically." Quentin seemed desperate now, somewhat crazed.

"Why, yes. When I've seen her, she's always been smiling and laughing." They took the pizza in the house and ate at the kitchen table.

"This Light person at the commune, where does he or she get the money to feed everybody?"

"I don't know. I'm never going back there. The Light spent its time telling us about the Supreme Being. The Friends of The Light handled the money."

"Why did Daydream want to leave?"

"The same reason I did. I came to believe The Light was a phony because it wouldn't let people leave when they wanted to."

Quentin threw the pizza box away, stood, and said, "I'm going to run and get some gas in the car." When he got out on the main road, he called the Menifee County Sheriff's Office. "Sir, did any of your men make a call early this morning to a farm up on Highway 36?"

"No. Who is this?"

"It must have been the state police. This is Quentin Lemaster. I live in Wrigley. Listen, I need for you to accompany me on a visit to 9400 Highway 36. I believe there are several people being held there against their will. One of them is my daughter, whom I haven't seen in seven years."

"Who told you that?"

"A young girl that escaped."

The sheriff began to press. "What's her name?"

"I don't know."

"Meet us here at our office at eight o'clock in the morning. Bring a picture of her and her birth certificate. We'll run over there and see what's going on." When Quentin reentered the house, he headed to the safe in his bedroom closet to open it. He pushed a few stacks of bills aside and sorted through a pile of papers until he found Carrie's birth certificate. He went into Carrie's old bedroom to retrieve the picture of her that Serenity had seen. He carefully dismantled the black picture frame and noticed that the combination to the safe was on the inside of the pasteboard backing. He remembered putting it there for Carrie in case she had to get into the safe for some reason. He took the frame and tucked it in the drawer of the table beside his bed.

Quentin and Serenity watched television shows and movies until after ten o'clock. He told her, "I'll be gone in the morning for a couple of hours. There's cereal, yogurt, and fruit in the kitchen for breakfast."

The Menifee County Sheriff's Office on Main Street in Frenchburg wasn't much. Two officers sat at a cheap folding table in the conference room, chomping on toothpicks, twirling them around, preparing to drive up into the forest in search of "The Light" and its prisoners. "We checked the property records. That land is in Boone Forest, and the government owns it. Any people in there will be squatters."

"Here's my daughter's picture and birth certificate," Quentin said as he tossed them across the table. Neither of the officers took the time to look at them.

The iron gates cut in the hill were still wide open, allowing both police cars to pull in and up the hill with ease. Once atop the ridge, wheel ruts became more overgrown and harder to navigate. The tracks got bumpier farther in. The men kept driving until it became clear that there wasn't anything or anybody back there in any direction. At a good turnaround spot, the three of them got out of the vehicles to discuss things. The talkative policeman of the two asked, "You want to tell us more about this?" He took his mangled toothpick and threw it in the grass.

"I guess the best thing to do is bring in the girl that gave me the address. She must have been mistaken," Lemaster said sheepishly.

"Go get her now. We'll be waiting at the office."

There was little traffic on that overcast Sunday morning, motivating Quentin to run twenty miles over the speed limit the whole way home. He stopped in the driveway and entered his house through the front door. After looking around, it was clear that Serenity had flown the coop.

Quentin hooked up his trailer and drove to the Paragon boat ramp. A stiff wind showed itself as choppy scallops on the surface of the water. A big "stinkpot" rumbled by and heaved the fishing boat as it approached the bridge. Quentin threw out the anchor by the spot where he had freed Serenity. He rigged up a thin rope with a large hook and sinker on it, threw it over the side, and began trying to snag the cable attached to the concrete block. Twenty minutes later, his arms were tired, and he was ready to give up. He finally got the tension and weight on the line he was looking for, reeling the bulky block up and out of the water. The brass wire looped through it had a hook and eye that would be easy to disconnect under water, which meant Serenity could have gotten loose with or without the help of good ole Quentin Lemaster.

On the way back to his house, Quentin called the Menifee County police to report that the girl stirring up all the trouble had taken off. Once inside the house, he stood close to the black safe in the bedroom closet, twisting the dial to unlock it. The door swiveled open and revealed that the fifty stacks of a hundred hundreds were gone. Well, that knocked everything into a cocked hat, he mused. Quentin let out a burst of deep, hearty laughter that ended in a coughing fit.

~ ~ ~

On Monday, the two girls sat in the sales office of a BMW dealership in Miami, waiting for the salesman to return with the paperwork for the Polestar 1 they had just agreed to purchase. He stepped back in the room and asked, "What name should we put on the title?"

"Serenity and Tranquility," one of the girls blurted, and then laughed. "I'm kidding. My name is Carrie Lemaster, and this is Sheila Broadbent. We want both names on it."

"Okay, and you said you were paying cash?"

"We are." Sheila put fifteen stacks of hundreds that came to $150,000 on the front of the desk.

The salesman said, "I'll write you a receipt." This was Miami. Anytime somebody tried to buy a BMW with cash, alarm bells went off. He took the money around the corner to the CFO, who checked the bills for authenticity. They were counterfeit. He called the police.

Five minutes later, two Miami police officers walked up behind the girls and made themselves known. "Both of you are under arrest for trying to pass counterfeit bills. Let's go down to the station," one of the policemen said.

Carrie looked at Sheila and jumped up. "What?"

"Your money is fake. That's a crime."

Sheila stood up too and spat, "I'll be a son of a bitch."

The detective sat in the interrogation room across from the two women. "So, where did you get this money?"

"From my father. Sheila took it out of his safe in the house I used to live in back in Kentucky."

"Does he know she took it?"

"Sure," Carrie said.

"What's his name?"

"Quentin Lemaster. He lives in the little burg of Wrigley."

The detective pushed the intercom and asked the data center to get Lemaster's phone number. In a few minutes, it was texted to him. The detective dialed the number and pressed the speaker button. "Hello. This is Quentin Lemaster."

"Mister Lemaster, this is the Miami police. I have your daughter and another girl here who say they got five hundred thousand dollars out of your safe yesterday. Is that the case?"

"A girl using the alias of Serenity took it, I believe."

"Who is Serenity?" The detective looked up to see Sheila's hand in the air.

"Well, sir, was that money counterfeit?"

"Wait a minute, officer. Does Serenity admit to taking the money?"

"Yes, I did," Sheila replied.

Quentin instructed, "Get both of them to sign a sworn statement to that effect and call me back." He hung up. It took a half hour to prepare the confession and get it signed by Sheila and Carrie.

"Now sir, is the money fake?"

"No. It was real. I don't know what they've done with the real money, but I want it back, or I'll press charges against them."

"Come on, Dad, why are you hanging us out like this?" Carrie moaned.

"Why did you run off? Why didn't you come visit your mother when she was sick? How come you didn't come to her funeral?" The pain in Quentin's voice was excruciating.

"I'm sorry, Dad. I know it was wrong." Tears popped in her eyes and ran down her cheeks. "Do you understand how lonely and depressing it is to live in the middle of nowhere? I almost lost my mind. I couldn't take it anymore. I'm sorry." Carrie dropped her face in her hands and cried audibly.

"You could have let us know you were all right. Your mother deserved better." The crying turned into full-blown sobbing. "Carrie, I can fix this if you and Serenity, or whatever her name is, come here and spend a little time with me. I want the chance to apologize for anything that I've done to hurt you."

Quentin Lemaster told the police detective how he had put the counterfeit money in his safe, hoping that his daughter would take it someday, spend it, and get caught. He was "baiting" her like a big fish to find out where she was. It worked, sort of.

After hanging up, he loaded the fishing boat with supplies for an evening of solitude on the lake. The vigorous wind would surely have the fish in a biting frenzy, he reflected. Tomorrow, the girls would be driving in from Florida for a visit. He wondered what Carrie would look like after being gone so long.

# THE BLACK TULIP

Nicholas "Nick" Lang surveyed the dining room at the Owensboro Country Club until he spotted Lorraine Keiper seated against the short wall next to the bank of windows overlooking the ninth green. She wore a gold-and-black striped A-line dress with three strands of black pearls around her bare neck. He rushed up and said, "Lorraine. What a pleasure to see you again. You're looking well."

"Thanks, Nick. Nice of you to come." She stood, gave him a pert hug, and gestured for him to sit across from her. "I took the liberty of ordering lunch for us, niçoise salads."

"Great. How long has it been, six or seven years?"

"Surely not that long," she said cheerfully.

"I moved to Louisville just over six years ago." Nick and Lorraine were good friends through high school, and went to Union College in Barbourville, Kentucky, together. The Keipers were wealthy, and the Langs weren't, but they became friends nonetheless. Neither married, and Nick signed on as a policeman when he returned to Owensboro after completing school. He later took a job as a private detective farther up the Kentucky River. Lorraine started seeing a man last spring who owned Aeolian Tulip Farm, located in the trendy little village of Tuck. He jilted her abruptly three weeks ago, hence her calling Nick.

"Time flies," she said. Lunch came, and they chatted casually over the pleasant meal. "Nick, I'm sure you know I asked you to lunch for something more than reminiscing."

"Well, in my business, this is how it usually starts. So, what's on your mind?"

"I would like to hire you to find out what's happened to Nelson Gillespie, a man I dated for a year. He dumped me recently, and now he's married to a woman named Kay Myrick. How could he do that?"

"Give me a few days, Lorraine, and I'll get some information for you," Lang assured her. They concluded their pleasantries, and he departed with his mind already spinning.

Aeolian Tulip Farm, by all indications, had developed into a thriving business. Nelson Gillespie seemingly had worked every foreseeable angle to make a buck. He sold live flowers and bags of bulbs like similar tulip operations, and had erected a picturesque tourist trap on the property. It was the only place in the state where an oenophile could buy a 4.25-ounce pour of Colgin Syrah, a very expensive California wine. Gillespie had also built a robust distribution network for bulbs. His usually sold out quickly due to their quality and consistency.

Nick Lang drove into the lot of Aeolian and parked his gray, ten-year-old Subaru in the back row. The acres of tulips were blooming in stripes of bright colors that were hard to appreciate unless actually seen in person. He stepped through the front door of the stone building to find the gift shop on the left, wine stand to the right, and seasonal outdoor gardens straight ahead. Wrought-iron tables and chairs were set up by the clusters of blooming flowers of every imaginable color except black.

Nick padded to the wine bar and asked, "Is Nelson Gillespie here today?"

"No, he isn't. I'm his wife. What can I do for you?"

"Oh, I just wanted to ask him if there was such a thing as a black tulip." He sized Kay up, taking in every detail—her grooming, figure, clothes, and brightness in her eyes.

"Why, yes. There is one variety. I don't think it is widely available though. We surely don't have it." She turned away to neatly stack stemware on a shelf. "Could I interest you in a glass of Colgin wine?"

"How much is it?" he questioned.

"Eighty dollars a pour." She spun back around to see if he was a big spender or not.

"I can't afford that," he replied playfully.

"What business are you in?"

"I'm a marriage counselor," he lied. "Are you in need of my services?"

"I sure hope not. I've only been hitched for a week," Kay Gillespie quipped.

Lang was the best at reading people, so good that he was absolutely sure something was rotten in Denmark.

"In that case, I'll take a tour of the gardens in search of other customers." He nodded at her as he backed away from the bar. Nick made a loop around the path through the flowers and went into the gift shop to see if there were any books on the farm's history. There weren't. He climbed into his car to start the drive back to Louisville.

The sleuthing business had become more about data mining than late-night stakeouts. Ordinary people knew how to get information on somebody, but it was the less-than-legal access to data that made Nick's time worth what he charged. The real secret to his success was the network of hackers at his disposal. He had a complete profile on Nelson Gillespie by eight that evening.

Gillespie, thirty-four, hailed from Horse Branch, Kentucky. He attended the University of Michigan Ross School of Business, got an MBA, and accepted a logistics job with the biggest flower wholesaler in the United States. He bought the tulip operation eight years back and left his corporate gig to manage the farm full time. He joined the Owensboro Country Club two years ago, where he met Lorraine Keiper at a cocktail party. By all accounts, Nelson Gillespie was an ordinary guy, on the boring side, with only one thing remotely suspicious in his record. According to his tax returns, which Nick had unlawfully looked at, Aeolian Tulip Farm had lost money every year.

Nick called Lorraine to give her a report. "There doesn't seem to be anything too interesting in Nelson's background. I did go out to the farm, and I met his wife, Kay. Did you ever meet her?"

"No," she said curtly.

"I'll check her out tomorrow and let you know what I find."

"When Nelson told me he couldn't see me anymore, he only said that a woman he had known for years had come back into his life, and that he had to work some things out with her."

The Kay Myrick who tended bar at the tulip farm didn't exist. There were nine people with that name in the United States. None fit the description of the woman he met. Nick hacked into the farm's payroll records, and the social security number in Kay's pay profile was for another person with that name, ninety years old, confined to a nursing home in New York. The address Kay had given for her residence was a spot on the south side of Owensboro, until it got changed to Nelson's place after they wed. She started working at the farm last fall and her paychecks had been cashed at the same liquor store near where she lived.

To get a marriage license in Kentucky, people present a birth certificate and provide their mother and father's names. Her full name was Kay Janetta Myrick, age thirty-five, born in Peoria, Illinois, to Samuel Myrick and Hortense Hatley, who didn't exist either.

Nick drove back downriver and arrived in Owensboro by noon.

The smell of Indian food was radiating through the cracked window of the manager's apartment. When the swarthy man opened the scuffed door, he spoke with a heavy accent. "Yes? How can I help you?" Orange specks of turmeric added an artistic flair to his frilly patterned shirt.

"I'm trying to get some information on Kay Myrick. I understand she rented an apartment here for a few months."

"That's right." He pulled a napkin from his pocket and mopped his lips and chin.

"What can you tell me about her?" Nick asked.

"Paid in cash on the first day of the month. Told me she was moving out and said to keep the security deposit."

"Did she ever have any visitors?"

"A man came by every evening to take some boxes from her car and put them in his trunk. I don't know what they were."

"Did you happen to see the license plate?"

"I think it was from the state of Washington."

Nick Lang wheeled into the parking lot of the white-painted, concrete-block liquor store that Kay Myrick visited once a week. The withered man at the counter, who appeared to have sampled his share of whiskey in his day, had a blue toothpick hanging from the corner of his mouth. "Do you remember the girl that came in here on Saturdays to get her checks cashed?"

"I do. What's it to you?" His chalky skin and hair looked as though dust might blow off them.

"She wanted me to give you this." Lang took a hundred-dollar bill from his shirt pocket.

"What for?"

"A little information," Nick replied as he placed the bill faceup by the register. "Did anyone ever come in here with her?"

"Her boyfriend." The man palmed the bill.

"Is this him?" Lang produced a picture of Nelson Gillespie.

"Nope. He looked like Johnny Carson when he was young."

"Thanks."

Nick went back out to his car to get on his laptop. He Googled Washington tulip farms to see if any of the faces were a match. Bingo. Carl Dunham, owner of Tiptoe between the Tulips, was a good likeness of Carson. One of the tulip varieties in his bulb catalog was black, not dark purple, but jet black. The note said, "SOLD OUT FOR THE SEASON."

"Lorraine? Hey, it's Nick. I think part of the puzzle has been solved."

"What have you learned?" she asked with excitement.

"Kay Myrick is not her real name. Two big questions remain: why did he marry her, and does he know who she really is?"

"Could it be blackmail?"

"More likely black tulips instead of blackmail."

"What do you mean?"

"I'll explain when I get a little more information," he said.

Lang called Carl Dunham. "I understand you spent a few weeks in Owensboro this winter. What brought you out here?"

"Well, Nelson Gillespie called me after Thanksgiving to tell me he'd gotten ahold of a solid black tulip. He knew I had been hoping to find one for years. He said he would sell the bulbs to me if I would come out and help him with a project."

"And that would be doing something with the boxes you pulled out of Kay Myrick's trunk every night."

"Hey, look, man, I swore I wouldn't tell anybody about that." Dunham became angry. A puff of exasperation came across the line.

"Cat's already out of the bag, and this might soon be police business." Nick sharpened his tone.

"All I did was drive the boxes to Evansville and give them to some mean-looking guy in a van. I did that for eighty-four days, and then Nelson sold me the black tulip bulbs. I headed home after that."

"Why did you go to the liquor store with Kay when she cashed her paychecks?"

"Because she would give me five hundred dollars a week in cash to live on. Told me I wasn't to use my credit card for anything."

"Were the boxes marked, or could you tell what was in them?" Lang asked.

"Plain cardboard, heavily taped. I don't know what they were."

"How many boxes were there?"

"Ten. Every night."

Nick did the math, 840 boxes of something valuable. There had to be some reason for whatever it was to be moved in small batches, he thought. Kay Myrick, now Gillespie, definitely knew why.

Kay was behind the counter at the wine bar when Lang entered Aeolian later that day. "Hello again," he offered as she moved a group of bottles onto a shelf, one by one.

"You here again?" She feigned disgust.

"Still trying to meet Nelson Gillespie. Is he here?"

"Sorry. Still gone."

"Is he ever coming back?"

"What kind of a crack is that?" Kay turned serious.

"That was uncalled for," Nick capitulated. "How can I make it up to you?"

"Buy an eighty-dollar glass of Colgin," she said.

"Okay, bring it on."

Kay grinned, pulled down the bottle to carefully measure the pour of 4.25 ounces that barely covered the bottom of the glass. "Here you go." The bottle had a simple rectangular label with basic burgundy foil on the neck.

Nick expected something special at that price. The wine seemed average to him. After draining the red liquid, he said, "That was good. Can I keep the glass as a souvenir?"

"Sure, for twenty dollars," she confirmed. He put down a hundred-dollar bill, clutched the glass, and saluted her on the way out.

He went straight to the Owensboro police lab and talked an old acquaintance into pulling prints off the wineglass. The tech ran them through the database and handed Nick a person's name. "Are you absolutely sure about this?" The tech nodded in the affirmative.

Nick had arranged to meet Lorraine Keiper at the Country Club for cocktails. When she arrived, he said, "You haven't changed a bit since we were in college. You look great."

She accepted the compliment graciously, replying, "Are you buttering me up for something?" Her robin's-egg blue blouse had an asymmetric neck that was hard not to stare at. They walked to the bar and ordered glasses of red wine.

"No, I just call 'em as I see 'em."

"So, what else have you found out?"

"I think Nelson Gillespie's gone missing, and his wife is into some sort of con."

"What do you mean gone missing?"

"Not around, and his wife won't tell me where he is. Kay is running ten cases of something over to Evansville every night, which leads me to believe she's moving stolen merchandise."

"Well, if you think he's really missing, shouldn't you go to the police?" Lorraine asked.

"Not yet. I want to clear something else up first."

Nick pulled into his favorite hacker's driveway at nine o'clock that evening. He asked the man to run the name Shannon Gillespie. He had information on her in less than five minutes. She was born in Horse Branch, Kentucky, and had a younger brother by the name of Nelson. She used a Masonville address on her last tax return, a spot in a little village right up the road from Aeolian Tulip Farm.

The next morning, Nick sat in his car near Shannon Gillespie's purported metal-building address in Masonville. A car pulled in and parked at the side door just after eight o'clock. The man, who Nick surmised to be Nelson Gillespie, got out and went inside empty-handed. Two hours later, he came back out to load ten case boxes into the car's trunk. He locked up and drove off slowly. Nick followed his vehicle until it turned in to the service road at the tulip farm.

Lang went back to Masonville and jimmied the lock. He looked around for thirty minutes before driving to a Mexican restaurant in downtown Owensboro. When he had finished eating, a call came in from Lorraine. "Nick, I just heard from Nelson."

"Did he tell you where he was?"

"Yep, at the tulip farm," she replied.

"What'd he say?"

"I'm not sure I believe him, but he told me why he cut things off between us. He said when he bought his farm eight years ago, he had borrowed the money to buy it from Kay Myrick."

"Oh, really?"

"Yes. He said he couldn't pay her back when the money was due, so she gave him two choices. He could either marry her, or she would foreclose on the property and seize it."

"Why'd he call to tell you that?" Nick asked.

"Because he said he sold a black tulip to a grower in Washington for two million dollars and that he'd paid Kay back. He claims she's agreed to give him a divorce. He also said she expressed an interest in buying the tulip farm from him."

"He should consider selling. He hasn't made the first nickel in that business," Nick told her.

"What do you mean?"

"I mean the guy hasn't made any money, except maybe from selling the black tulip, and I'm not so sure about that. Look, Lorraine, why don't we catch dinner, and I'll share with you what I've found out."

She suggested, "The Mason Grill at six thirty."

"I'm going to run home for a bit. See you tonight."

One thing wasn't squaring with him on the ride to Louisville. He went to the computer in his house and pulled up the website for Tiptoe between the Tulips. He scanned the photo gallery and found what he was looking for.

~ ~ ~

Lorraine Keiper had on a beautiful wrap dress with pewter zig-zags and diamond stud earrings. Nick looked sharp in his tight-fitting silver blazer and purple tie. He asked the waiter, "Do you have Colgin wine here?"

"We do, sir. I believe a bottle is seven hundred eighty-five dollars."

"Bring that, please." The waiter nodded and smiled. Nick turned to Lorraine and said, "I'll add it to your bill. We're celebrating."

"What, pray tell?"

"The sudden good fortune of your ex-boyfriend. He will likely be coming back to you, but this time with a seven-figure bank account."

"I'm not so sure I want him back," she said.

The wine came, and it was complex, having overtones of dark berries, flowers, and licorice. Nick looked at it and commented, "Now, this is the real deal."

"What are you talking about?"

"I'll start at the beginning. Nelson Gillespie decided a couple of years ago that he wanted to run with the country club crowd. The only problem was he didn't have the kind of cash you need to do that. He'd done nothing but lose money in tulips, but then last summer, his sister, who he'd not seen or heard from for years, called him with an interesting proposition."

Lorraine buttered a piece of bread and said, "He didn't tell me he had a sister."

"Her name is Shannon Gillespie. She works for Carl Dunham at a tulip farm in Washington, but goes by the name Kay Myrick. Dunham was just as broke as Nelson last summer. Carl decided he wanted to start counterfeiting expensive wines to make money, and the priciest of them all is right there." He pointed in the direction of the bottle of Colgin. "And the beauty of it is, the label and foil are remarkably easy to copy."

"Why in the world did he marry his sister?"

"Well, Nelson wanted to cash out of the tulip business, Carl Dunham needed to get some dough to buy the black tulips, and Shannon planned to get control of Nelson's farm. She became Kay Myrick, and with the bogus marriage to Nelson, her name could be put on the deed."

"How did this fake wine business turn out?"

"They were putting cheap wine in one hundred and twenty bottles a day over in Masonville at some building owned by Shannon, alias Kay. They were careful to work in small quantities. It would be possible to fill fifteen thousand bottles in one hundred twenty-five days. If they could net two hundred a bottle, or more, you're talking at least three million."

Lorraine let out a long, slow whistle. "Who's got that money?"

"Shannon would have given her cut to Nelson to buy the farm, and Carl would have bought the black tulips from Nelson with his. I'd say your boy is out of flowers and into fake wines, walking around with three million dollars in his pocket. He can run with the clubbers now."

"You're more my kind of boy, Nick. Shall we order dinner?" She put her hand on his.

"I guess you expect me to pay for this wine." He rubbed her hand softly with his thumb.

"It's cheaper than buying me a black tulip." She raised her glass to him.

# Unrequited Love for Falcons and King

On April 26, 2011, tornadoes ripped through Tar Hill, Kentucky, cutting a swath a quarter-mile wide and three miles long. Ezra King figured a storm like that never hit the same spot twice, so he bought up forty acres of cheap land and put in thirty acres of grapevines, half cabernet sauvignon and the rest chardonnay. He didn't get much of a crop the first three years, but by year five, the grapes were piled up everywhere, which compelled him to build a picturesque wine operation in the middle of nowhere. Ezra took a flyer and aged his initial batch in used bourbon barrels from Wild Turkey Distillery for the last sixty days of maturation. The first bottling of 4,000 cases got snapped up before he could set the right price. Apparently, it wasn't enough.

The wine critics ran across a few bottles by late 2018 and rated the stuff as the best on Planet Earth. Talk about angry, the Napa Valley vintners could scarcely disguise their disdain for the Kentucky hill jack whose wine had shot to the top of the chart. Something had to be done, but what exactly?

Ezra King was producing 6,000 cases a year by 2021, and would only sell his sought-after brand in four-case lots, two white and two red, at $416.67 a bottle. That made each order a nice round $20,000. If he could have sold it all, we'd be talking $30 million. Unfortunately, he only moved 1,000 cases at that price, still a good chunk of money, but he was banking on demand firming up in future years. An enormous climate-controlled warehouse went in next to the winery, and 5,000 cases languished there, waiting for crazy people to swing through and pay the ridiculous price.

Ezra's wife, Victoria, dropped a million on a pristine house at the edge of the vineyard. It had all the bells and whistles of a city residence, allowing her to entertain wine aficionados stopping by, trying to figure out how Ezra pulled off such a remarkable feat in a mere ten years. She surprised her husband with a new metallic green Porsche 911 Carrera to affirm his success. Victoria made the factory omit the car's satellite tracking equipment, which meant it could not be located on the road. Ezra appreciated the stealth nature of that feature, even though the convenience of a built-in GPS would be missed at times.

Thirty people now worked at the winery full time, and Ezra King gave them all lavish bonuses at the end of the year. He enjoyed delivering wine to customers in his Porsche, providing him the excuse to whoosh around the backroads of Kentucky. All seemed well, but as could have been predicted, trouble was brewing. Every critter in the state had heard about the succulent grapes on old man King's farm. Sparrows, robins, starlings, grackles, black-birds, and wild turkeys flew in and were feasting away, not to mention the deer, foxes, raccoons, rabbits, squirrels, and every other varmint that was sneaking around amid the vines. Soon, there wouldn't be any grapes left, ergo no wine gravy train.

King contacted the U.S. Fish and Wildlife Service and got a list of General and Master Falconers. He searched each name on the Internet, looking for someone in the pest abatement business. There were only a handful of contacts, all on the West Coast, mostly in Napa Valley. He started by phoning the one that advertised specializing in vineyard protection. "This is Ezra King calling. I've got a wine business in the middle of Kentucky that desperately needs to scare off a boatload of pests."

The man on the other end said, "Sorry, sir, I can't help you with that. My birds don't travel that far."

"Well, can you give me any suggestions?"

"As a matter of fact, I can. I mentored a nice young girl for two years until she got her General designation in falconry, and I believe she just got her Masters recently. The last time I talked to her, she said she wanted to move back to Kentucky. She mentioned the town of Leitchfield."

"That's ten miles from my vineyard," King replied with excitement.

"Her name is Tori Pincus. I'll text her phone number to you. If you hire her, call me back, and let me know how she works out."

"So, what's the setup with falcons, and how much do they cost?" King asked.

"How many acres of vines do you have?"

"Thirty."

"It will require two birds rotating from sunup to sundown along with a dog. I'm pretty sure Tori has a vizsla, and I know she has two falcons. I helped her catch and train them."

"Will the person need to live on the property?"

The falconer responded, "Out here, the vintners build small houses with dog pens and two large mews that have perches, smooth walls, and steel bars. Each mew has an anteroom to keep the falcons from taking off."

"Sounds like a fifty-grand proposition before I even get started," King said despondently.

"That ain't the half of it, partner. You'll need protection during growing season, from Memorial Day till Halloween, at a thousand dollars a day. You can pencil in a hundred and fifty on top of the fifty for next season. I hope you're getting a pretty penny for your wine."

King reluctantly told him, "North of four hundred dollars a bottle."

The falconer said, "Holy smokes," before ringing off.

King made a deal with Pincus right after Thanksgiving and had her tell him what kind of facility to build on the property. She worked up plans and specifications detailing living quarters for her falcons, Eurus and Pan, and Brizo, the dog. Ezra promised to have it completed by mid-May. Tori agreed to work the growing season through harvest, from June 1 until October 31. She planned to find work back in California from November to May to finally make the years of training birds and dogs pay off.

When the storms went through in 2011, Tori Pincus was a month from graduating with honors from Grayson County High School. She knew all the kids in her class who lived in Tar Hill. Many of their homes were damaged. It was hard to reconcile those days with the opportunity given her to return there, to work at Tar Hill Winery, now world renowned. As like most things in life, timing is everything. She had dropped out of college after two years to pursue her passion of becoming a Master Falconer. She knew it was a seven-year proposition, but had the stick-to-itiveness to see it through. She found a mentor in California and learned the pest abatement business from him.

The seven years of learning falconry were an unspeakable grind. She had to capture the young birds and then spend endless hours teaching them to be comfortable around her. The nonstop training, based on the positive reinforcement of food, kept her incessantly cutting up mice and chicken. At first, the falcons were tethered. Next, a homing device was planted in their wings, and finally, they had to be trained to go places and pursue things on their own. The hardest part of it was the unrequited love. She loved the birds, but they certainly did not love her. Falcons were not like dogs. They would be just as happy to fly off and never see their handler again.

Tori pulled the van up to the front of Tar Hill Winery, expecting Ezra King to emerge and meet her. He did not disappoint. She thought him to be handsome in a rugged way, the kind of man she would like to have or at least work for. Tori rolled down the window and chirped, "I take it you're Mister King. Where should I unload the family?"

"I'll get in with you, and we'll ride over together." Tori looked pretty much as he expected her to, physical and outdoorsy. "Go back out on the main road to the next driveway. Your Taj Mahal is in the middle of the vines, up on a hill." She grinned and dropped the van in reverse.

As they approached the aviary-slash-kennel-slash-boardinghouse, Tori blurted, "Oh, man, this place is absolutely beautiful!"

King asked, "Do you need any help unloading?"

"No. You'd spook the birds."

"Okay, then, I'll walk back to the winery. After you get settled, please join my wife and me for dinner at our house. We're happy you're here." He nodded and gave her a genial smile.

Tori spent the rest of the day getting the falcons and dog acclimated to their new surroundings. Her living quarters were fully furnished and stocked with food, including a bottle each of Tar Hill red and white. She got cleaned up before opening them. They were indeed spectacular.

Dinner at the King house was delightful. Victoria knew how to entertain and "walk the dog." When Tori strode toward her van after supper, she turned around to make sure Ezra and Victoria had closed the door behind her. She pulled something out of her jeans pocket and slid underneath the rear of the Porsche to quickly mount it on the car where it would be hard to see or find. When she got inside her new house, she checked the homing device's receiver to make sure the one she had put on King's car was transmitting. Her mentor in California taught her that trick. It was always good to know where the boss man was.

It took Eurus and Pan the month of June to get down the routine of flying over the vineyard and shooing away the unwanted fauna. Brizo patrolled the rows of vines when the falcons rested on their perches. A few nights a week, Tori would invite relatives or high school friends to come by for supper and a movie. All the men she had been interested in, before leaving town years ago, were spoken for now, which only helped fuel her affection for Ezra King. He was eighteen years older than she was and married. The way things were going, she might have to give up her cushy gig after one season and move back to California permanently to keep her sanity.

At quitting time for the help, Tori Pincus went over to the winery on a Friday in early August to see what the customer traffic was like. She spotted Ezra in the warehouse loading cases of wine into the trunk of his Porsche. When she approached him, he said, "I'm going to make a run over to Louisville. Two restaurants have bought orders of the 2018 vintage. One of them asked me to stay for dinner. I should be back by eleven." He shut the trunk and looked at Tori with a critical eye. "I'm thinking of raising the price on the inventory that's left."

"Why not, if you can get it," she replied. Tori watched him pull away in a cloud of dust.

The winery closed at five o'clock. The last two couples to leave were carping about the price of Tar Hill wine as they piled into an SUV. Tori and Victoria chatted for a few minutes, and then Victoria said, "I need to get out of here. I'm meeting a friend for dinner in Elizabethtown."

Tori turned Brizo loose to run the vineyard and went inside to check Ezra's homing device. His car was parked in a field on the other side of the highway, not more than a quarter mile up the road. It stayed there for nearly half an hour before moving again in the direction of Louisville.

Brizo went back in his cage while Tori sent Eurus out. He returned promptly and landed on her leather-clad arm. He instantly dispatched the chicken offered as the reward for a job well done. Pan made his run a little before dark. Ezra's car had been parked in Louisville for nearly three hours and was on the move again, ostensibly returning home. Tori pushed the homing receiver aside and turned on the TV.

Tori saw Victoria's car pulling in the driveway of the King house at ten o'clock. She checked the homing device again to see that Ezra's car was in the field across the road again. She shut off all the lights and TV, and sat by the window facing the lane. The Porsche pulled in thirty minutes later.

Ezra King walked up the hill on Saturday morning where he located Tori with Eurus on her arm. The fresh air felt crisp and the scent of grapes wafted faintly through. His downcast expression prompted her to ask, "Something the matter?"

"When I got home last night, Victoria's car was in the driveway, but she wasn't in the house."

"I saw her drive in at around ten last night." Tori gave the command for the falcon to take flight.

"She must have left with somebody," he said.

"I didn't see any other cars."

King did a circle in place, following the path of the falcon. "Look, I've got problems. Victoria told me that she wanted a divorce and wants to buy my half of the winery. Says she's taken up with a guy from Napa Valley."

"Oh, really. Who would that be?"

"I don't know who it is, but I'll bet it's the way they've conjured up to get rid of me. I've caused too much trouble for the California crowd," he said doggedly.

"Well, one thing is for sure, to get a divorce, she'll have to show up again. She doesn't strike me as mean-spirited." Tori had Ezra cornered, but he didn't know it yet. "So, if she stays gone, would you consider taking an interest in a younger woman?"

"What are you talking about?" he asked, completely perplexed.

"I'm talking about me." She gazed at him with a loving smile.

"Surely I'm too old for you." He looked up at the falcon again.

"I don't think so," she rebutted.

"I'm flattered, but can't think about that now."

Ezra watched as Tori raised her arm signaling for the bird to land on it. She gave him part of a mouse on the trip back to his perch in the mew. She came back out and said, "I'll be waiting if she doesn't come back."

It was plain to see by September that there would be a bumper crop of grapes that year. Ezra shared openly that he thought his wife had left him for another man. The wine press conjured up conspiracy theories and printed stories pitting the Kentucky rube against the elites of Napa Valley. All that did was increase the demand for Tar Hill wines. The search for Victoria reached a fever pitch.

Tori Pincus crept along the lane in her van, looking for any place to turn off into the field on the other side of the road. There were two ruts passable by car, so she wheeled onto them and proceeded to a wooded section, about 300 yards in. She got out to inspect the grounds.

Tori returned to the winery to find King after forty-five minutes. She asked him, "Okay if I come by your house after five o'clock? I've got something I need to tell you."

He hesitated before answering, "Sure."

Ezra let Tori in the house at 5:10. "Can I get you anything?" he asked. She declined, and they sat across from each other in the front room.

"I figured out how you did it," she stated.

"Did what?"

"Killed Victoria."

"What are you talking about?" King bounced around on the sofa cushion and clasped his hands.

"You knew that she was going to Elizabethtown after you left for Louisville, so you pulled into the field and stood by the road until she came along. She stopped when she saw you, and you must have Tased her or something. Then you drove her car back in the woods and buried her."

"That's ridiculous," he spat.

"You went on to Louisville, and when you got back, you pulled into the woods to drive her car to the house. You walked back to your car and drove it in thirty minutes later."

"How in the world did you come up with such a tale? I went to Louisville, dropped the orders off, had dinner, and came home. You can check that out," he replied high-handedly.

"You know that falcons have homing devices in their wings, right?"

"Well, yes."

"I stuck one on your Porsche when I first saw the car. I followed your trail the night you killed her. And, I saw where you buried her." She got up and stared down at him. "So, there are two ways you can handle this, with money or love. I prefer the latter." Tori left the house quietly. After she had been gone for three minutes, Ezra searched the underside of his car systematically until he found where she had placed the device. He crushed it with the heel of his boot, went into the house, grabbed a hunting knife, and started in the direction of Tori's cabin.

"Come in," she said when King knocked on the door.

He stepped inside to see her sitting serenely in an Adirondack chair with one of the falcons on her gloved right hand. "Ah, Ezra, nice of you to stop by so soon. I see it didn't take you long to make up your mind."

"I know this. You can't prove anything."

"What about the body?"

"I'll move it and deny I had anything to do with her death." He sniffed and wiped the sweat off his forehead.

"You understand that if I give the command, this bird will maul you. I'd be polite if I were you."

"You're crazy," he retorted.

Tori stood suddenly and yelled, "Kill!" The falcon flapped its wings violently and began to fly around the room erratically. It became disoriented, made awful screeching noises before finally turning on her. King shot toward the exit. She put her arms in front of her face and cried for help. He slammed the door and ran to call for an ambulance and the police.

The ambulance was still in front of Tori's house when the state trooper knocked on Ezra's door. "Are you Ezra King?"

"Yes. How is she?"

"She's dead, sir," the trooper reported soberly. "So you ran out. What did she tell you before that?"

King's face tipped off the fact that he was trying to figure out what to say. "Well, she said she killed my wife, and buried her in a field across the road."

"For what reason?"

"Jealousy, I guess. She wanted me for herself." That second part was true, but didn't seem to wave the policeman's stern expression.

The state trooper pulled a voice recorder from his pocket. "I've not been truthful with you, Mister King. Miss Pincus called off the falcon, and she's doing fine." He tossed the recorder on the coffee table and said, "Your confession is on here. I'm going to arrest you for the murder of your wife."

Tori barged in the house in a huff and declared, "Too bad, Ezra, you had a good thing going. I'll make sure the pests don't ruin this year's crop." He looked down, put his face in his hands, and made a growling sound that grew into a full-blown scream.

# IT MIGHT BE TIME TO CAVE

Rosella Mansfield had been putting off investigating the sinkhole fenced in by the last owner of the unorthodox horse farm that now belonged to her, but it was time, and she had conjured up the nerve to do it. Rosella deposited the horses in the barn and drove the muddy blue Jeep over the hill to the back of the pasture where the small, circular V-mesh fence with a curved wooden top rail stood like a shrine to some UFO that had burned a scar in the ground. She used two ladders, one on each side, to scale the fence with ease. Several rolls of rusted wire had been tossed into the hole to block entry, and that almost dissuaded her from going any further.

It took Rosella a while to descend the shaft through the tangled web of gnarly orange bales. She unhooked the flashlight from her belt, turned it on, and cast the beam into the abyss below. It's what she had feared most, an entrance to a cave.

Woodford County, Kentucky, just west of Keeneland, had some of the best farmland and horse farms in all the world. It also had its share of decrepit tumble-downs owned by families on the margins, as peasants around castles. Rosella's tiny spread that she bought six months ago was well kept, but quirky in design. The green-and-white barn behind the house followed convention. However, what should have been the back porch was, curiously, the front porch of the house. The white-brick façade had an alcove floored in big red flagstone and wrapped with vegetation gardens. The redwood trellis bolted onto the brick levitated over the entrance. Wall-mounted planters were filled with succulents, and the teakwood furniture consisted of a round table, four chairs, two loungers, and side tables. The dark green cushions matched the trim color of the barn. Next to the front door, the farm's horse-racing silks of red, green, and white pulled the decorating scheme all together.

The farm to the north, by contrast, was conventional, a symmetrical yellow colonial home with dormers, columns, and notable soffits and fascia. The professional landscaping featured a blend of magnolias, dogwoods, and hardy shrubs. The porch and circular driveway, paved with brown brick, had lighting that made the place look like a fancy restaurant at night. Morris Bentz took possession of it after he got out of jail a year ago. He served three and one-half years of a six-year sentence for killing his now ex-wife's boyfriend.

Rosella stepped down through the entrance to the cave into a damp area that had stalagmites and stalactites the color of coffee with two creams. The water dripping from the ceiling made unsettling plunk and splat sounds. She played the light over the bristly walls for several minutes in search of a passage leading somewhere. There was a hole in the wall by the floor to the right. She would have to crawl. Rosella took a deep breath, exhaled in fear, and got down on her stomach to shine the light ahead. The clearance was plenty wide, but only a foot and one-half high. She began crawling with the light out in front of her and, after fifteen feet, saw that the gap had narrowed to being impassable. She banged the light on the ceiling, and it flickered out. Everything went black. Rosella panicked, shook the light vigorously, and it shined dimly again. She backed out as quickly as possible, ran to the way out, and began scrabbling up through the wire fencing. As she broke free, the sunshine and hot wind felt good on her face.

Sara Lannefors owned one of the larger and more prosperous horse farms in Woodford County until she died three years ago. Her heirs sold the place to an Arabian contingency and donated her marvelous collection of rare Waterford crystal to the town of Versailles with the stipulation that a small museum be started in her name on North Main Street. Lannefors Crystal Museum opened to the enjoyment of brisk traffic from Bourbon Trail sightseers. It had one piece valued at $800,000, worth more than the rest of the collection in total, a 1799 flint-glass goblet made for George Washington. Henry Clay bought the goblet in 1812 and gave it to his wife Lucretia as a gift because it was made the year they were married. It now sat on a pedestal in the center of the one-room museum as the featured attraction. Many of the other pieces had been made for the horse racing industry. There were enlarged pictures of related events on the walls.

Rosella's front porch faced east toward the morning sun. When the weather was good, she ate Greek yogurt and fruit out there, drank green tea, and read the *Lexington Herald-Leader*. A blurb caught her attention:

> *On Tuesday around four o'clock in the morning, the power to Lannefors Crystal Museum in Versailles was cut, rendering the alarm system ineffective. Thieves broke in and removed the prized goblet once owned by George Washington and Henry Clay. Police are checking video cameras up and down Main Street looking for leads that might identify the culprits. Anyone having information about the robbery is urged to contact the Versailles Police Department.*

Rosella jiggled her head and turned to yesterday's race results at Churchill Downs on the back page of the sports section. After she finished reading, she put her hands on her thighs and drew a full breath. Today, she would take another crack at the cave under the sinkhole.

She started by taking a closer look at the walls of the main cavern near the entrance. This time she had three flashlights. On the far side, the spiny floor sloped up and tapered into the ceiling. She stepped through to the other side, where she saw a round hole about two feet in diameter, high up on the wall. Rosella launched headfirst through the small hole into a rough-hewn tunnel comfortable for walking. She switched off the flashlight to experience absolute black. It seemed peaceful, and suddenly, a confidence came over her, similar to what scuba divers experience when the surface is so far away that it loses its relevance. She turned the flashlight back on and moved along without caution. After what seemed a quarter of a mile, she turned it off again. Dim light could be seen ahead, signaling another way out.

There was a cutback at the dead end of the tunnel that revealed the source of the light. Rosella squeezed through a narrow vertical breach in the wall to find herself on the backside of a wine cellar. The shelving had been affixed to the walls, so the only way to get into the middle would be to remove a diagonal stack of wine bottles and squirm through. She carefully lifted bottles and set them behind the shelf and once again crawled forward. When Rosella got through and stood in the dim emergency lighting, she saw it, the stolen crystal goblet. She clutched it in her hand, retreated, and restacked the wine. She took the bottle on top with her, a 2014 Screaming Eagle Sauvignon Blanc.

Morris Bentz opened the front door of his house to see four uniformed police officers standing together on the stoop with stern looks on their faces. Three of them could have stood to lose forty pounds. The man in front asked, "Are you Morris Bentz?"

"I am."

"We have a warrant to search your house." He slapped the paperwork in Morris's hand before pushing him aside and entering the main hallway. The other men followed closely behind.

"What's this about?"

"We have a video of a Corvette registered to you that drove through downtown in this direction at a little after four in the morning last Tuesday. We're looking for a stolen goblet."

Bentz contemplated his next move, but said nothing. The men spent fifty minutes rummaging through the upstairs, and then one of them turned the knob on the wine cellar door to no avail. "Where's the key to this?" he asked.

Bentz said, "I'm not sure, I never go down there."

The lead officer said, "I'll call the locksmith to come drill it out." He pulled a cell phone from his back pocket.

"Let me go look for it," Bentz replied. He returned with the key in several minutes. He unlocked the door, turned on the light, and proceeded ahead of the men down the stairs. He was hoping by some miracle that the stolen goblet no longer sat on the table at the center of the racks, and to his astonishment, it was, in fact, gone. Morris Bentz couldn't believe his luck.

The police were disappointed not to find anything. Bentz said to them as they were leaving, "I don't have it. Good day, men." He was telling the truth.

One of the policemen whirled around, examined Morris suspiciously, and said, "Don't go down there much, huh? Must be eighty thousand dollars in wine on those shelves." He waited for the other men to get out the door before averting his stare and leaving himself.

Bentz shot back down the wine cellar steps after the police drove off to figure out what the hell was going on. Someone must have broken in and taken the goblet. But how? He was ready to ascend the stairs again when he noticed that the top bottle on the wine pyramid in a cubicle on the left wall was missing. It was one thing for a stolen object to disappear, another for wine he paid $1,000 for to go poof.

At quitting time for first-shift workers, Morris Bentz drove his white Corvette onto the driveway of Rosella Mansfield's farm. He saw her sitting on the porch, feet up on a chair, holding a glass of white wine. He parked as close to the house as he could, got out, and waved in her direction. "Hello there," he said.

Rosella got to her feet and strolled over to him. "Hi. What can I do for you?" she asked.

"Morris Bentz. I live next door. Thought I ought to come by and introduce myself." He nodded sheepishly and broke into a jittery smile.

"Care to join me on the porch for a glass of wine?"

"Thank you." Morris Bentz always wondered if people knew his story, and to get that behind him, he usually told them about it as soon as an opportunity arose. "I didn't know the people here before you. I've only been in Kentucky for about a year."

"What brought you here?" she asked.

"The romantic notion of owning a horse farm. When I first toured these parts, I was sure it was the center of the universe." Bentz traipsed over to look carefully at the racing silks mounted by the door.

Rosella went into the kitchen and returned with two full glasses of white wine. She dug in further with "Well, these places take money, so how are you earning yours?"

"I'm a treasure hunter." Rosella half choked on her wine and covered her mouth. "Don't laugh. I dive shipwrecks." He sipped the wine she gave him and peered at it incredulously. "Wow, this is really good wine. What's the name of it?"

"Screaming Eagle. The man who sold me the house left it here. Pretty good, wouldn't you say?" Morris knew damn well she was lying. That was his wine, and somehow, she had stolen it. That meant she had the goblet too. He tried to process everything in his mind.

"It's better than good. More like a thousand dollars good."

"I thought you might like it," she replied.

Bentz changed course and offered, "There's more about me you should know." He sat down next to her facing the front yard and shifted in his seat. "I got out of prison a year ago. I was convicted of killing my wife's boyfriend. I didn't do it. She's my ex-wife now."

"If you didn't kill him, who did?"

"My wife. She wore gloves when she shot him with my gun. It was her word against mine. My prints were on the pistol, so they pinned it on me."

Rosella tried to lighten the mood by saying, "Nice wife you had there. No wonder she's gone."

"Tell me about it," he muttered. "Hey, listen, I came over for another reason. Someone broke into my house in the last couple of days. I was hoping that you might have seen something or someone snooping around."

"Sorry, I didn't notice anything except the cop car that was there. You report it to the police?"

"Uh, yeah." Bentz took the last sip from his glass and stood to leave. "Well, it has been great to meet you. Please stop over my place any time."

"I will. Oh, by the way, I have a question for you. I've got a goblet that's over two hundred years old, and since you're in the treasure business, you must know a discreet person I can sell it to." She batted her eyes unassumingly.

*Now we're getting down to business*, he thought. "I'm sure I do. How much exactly do you want for the piece?"

"Three hundred thousand."

"Come over to my house in the morning, and I'll have the cash ready for you," he said.

"I've got a better idea. Get the cash now. Bring it here. I'll hand you the goblet, right out in broad daylight. That way there's no funny business."

Bentz got in his Corvette, drove to the bank before it closed, loaded the money from a lockbox into a briefcase, and returned to Mansfield's farm to make the swap.

~ ~ ~

Rosella Mansfield hoofed it over to Morris Bentz's farm the next morning and knocked on the door. He answered and ushered her in with widened eyes. "You are full of surprises," he said. "What do you want now, all the wine in my cellar?"

"No, I came by to tell you about the escape tunnel down there." She turned and looked out the front window to see police cars pulling into his driveway and hers. "What do they want?" She pointed. He joined her to see who it was. She rubbed the side of her neck and said, "They're looking for something. Quick, get me a flashlight, give me the goblet, and lock me in the wine cellar."

Morris firmly latched the cellar just before the knock came. He waited as long as he could before opening the door. The policeman said, "We have an amended warrant here to search an escape tunnel in your wine cellar. Open up." The policeman glared at the doorknob.

"I'll get the key." When he returned, he stated, "I don't know about any secret passage down there."

The policeman replied, "I called the previous owner of this farm. He told me where to find it." Two other officers followed him down the steps after he turned on the light. They immediately saw the cubicle where the wine bottles had been taken out. "I'll see what's back here. You guys keep an eye on Bentz." He switched on a big flashlight and crawled halfway through the rack. In a few seconds, he yelled, "Wait! I'm too fat to fit through here." He backed out and told Bobby, "Go back there and look for anything or anybody. It leads to a sinkhole on the farm next door. I sent Tucker over there to block it off."

When Rosella got to the cave exit, she could see the police officer standing above the bales of wire, rifle hanging loosely in his right hand. Behind her was the beam of light coming from the hole that connected the tunnel to the cave. Carrying the goblet box, she got down and crawled into the slot she had been in when her light had gone out. Rosella wriggled in as far as she could this time, nearly twenty feet. The clearance was barely a foot. She switched off the flashlight to face total darkness.

After about twenty minutes, she saw a shaft of light sweep across the entrance to the crevice she was in. A voice could be heard announcing, "Tucker, I've checked everything. There's nothing or nobody down here. I'm coming out." She lay there for another hour, in a trance, before testing the flashlight. It came on. She climbed up through the wire slowly, making sure that the police had left.

Rosella headed straight for her blue Jeep after debouching from the sinkhole. She took a Magic Marker from the console to write an address on the box that held the goblet, and drove to the post office to mail it. She returned home, took a shower, fixed a sandwich, and sat on the front porch to decompress. Morris Bentz wheeled into Rosella's driveway after she was done eating. He jumped out and asked, "What did you do with it?"

"I sent it to you certified mail." He acted nonplussed. "So, Morris, who is your fence?"

"My ex-wife."

"What?"

"Yeah, that's how we met and got married in the first place. I took her some treasure to dispose of discreetly."

Rosella said, "So that tells me you're the one who shot her boyfriend, not her. Am I right?"

Bentz's face became immobile with a vacant gaze. "She paid me a half million in cash to get rid of the bastard. He was extorting her. She insisted that we get a divorce to make it look legit." Rosella picked up her empty plate and glass without saying a word. He pleaded, "That doesn't mean I love her anymore. Actually, I've grown fond of you since we met." She burbled in anger as she stepped through the front door, slamming it shut with her foot.

~ ~ ~

Rosella Mansfield opened the *Louisville Courier-Journal* three weeks later and saw the small report:

> *The goblet taken from the Lannefors Crystal Museum a month ago has been recovered on Long Island. It was among the effects of Madeline Bentz, an import-export merchant shot and killed early Tuesday morning. The police have long suspected her to be a fence for recovered treasure and stolen goods. Her ex-husband, Morris Bentz, lives on a farm in Versailles, Kentucky, and is considered a suspect in the killing. He remains at large. Anyone having any information as to his whereabouts is urged to contact the Versailles Police Department.*

Rosella threw the paper on the ground and let out a cute-girl laugh. She shielded her eyes and squinted from the sun. It was going to be another hot one. Time to steal more of Bentz's wine before it got impounded, while the morning was still cool, before the police found out he was never coming back.

# ROBILLARD'S DIPTYCH

"Damn it, Donovan, where's my Martini?" Irwin Robillard shook his baggy face in anger, causing saliva to seep from the corners of his mouth down onto his chin. He savagely wiped away the spittle with the sleeve of his tattered dress shirt before licking his lips.

"What are you talking about, Dad?" His son didn't quite know how to handle his addlepated, eighty-eight-year-old father, who had become increasingly paranoid over the last few months. Suddenly, the vignettes of the two of them in that room came flooding back, the most poignant being the time he had sassed his mother. He heard a diatribe that day from his dad on respect. There were plenty of good times to remember, but they seemed hollow at the moment.

"My Martini. You stole it." Irwin levered himself up out of the ninth or tenth version of the recliner that had been in that same spot for the last sixty-five years. The simple limestone house in the Lansdowne development, where Donovan and his older sister Thekla grew up, had been Irwin's home and his convivial wife, Bunny's, since they were both twenty-three years old. Bunny passed on a year ago. Irwin had turned dour since her death and didn't intend to move into a nursing home. He wanted to stay in the only house he'd ever owned, a predicament that would have to be dealt with by his children sooner than later.

"I did not. You gave it to me for safekeeping." That was a lie, yet no one could prove otherwise.

"Well, I want it back." Irwin stood erect and warily shuffled over to within a foot of Donovan's face. He knew his son was flat broke. In the end, it was Donovan who brought down Mountain Central Life, the business that his lifelong friend, Dawson "Sonny" Blankenship, had built into an empire.

"Okay, Dad, I'll return it. I don't know why you're getting so worked up."

"Because I want my Martini!" Irwin Robillard intended to find out what his wrecking ball of a son was up to.

## SEVENTY YEARS AGO

Irwin grew up in Lexington's imperial Cherokee Park neighborhood. He made good enough grades in high school to get into college, but fought shy of the University of Kentucky, a mere mile north of where he lived. Irwin decided on Eastern Kentucky University instead, hoping to make friends there, something he had not done heretofore. That's where he first met Sonny Blankenship.

Sonny came from a well-heeled Eastern Kentucky family. His social sphere included people like Robillard, those he could effortlessly manipulate and control. Irwin was introverted and guarded with his feelings. Blankenship noticed that and had the decency not to trample on the man's emotions.

A room always lit up when Sonny came into it. He was dynamic, fearless, and driven. He wasted little time finding his future wife, Marta, and triumphantly orchestrated the courtship between Marta's roommate, Bunny Toland, and his friend Irwin. Bunny ran pretty rich and added that needed spark to the solemn Robillard. After graduation, the four of them had a donnish wedding that Irwin barely got through without having a nervous breakdown.

Sonny Blankenship felt responsible for Irwin's well-being, so he talked his affluent father into putting up the cash to buy a country auction company west of Richmond, located in a good spot to pull in crowds from the interstate highways and urban districts. Robillard was offered the position of general manager, and it would be the only job he would ever have.

The business turned a profit the first year, compelling Sonny to give Irwin a bonus that he used as a down payment on a house in the peaceful suburb southeast of Lexington. As long as the Blankenships owned the auction company, Robillard drove to Richmond when it was open, some fifty-five years, until he had to retire at the age of seventy-eight. That was ten years ago, and nothing but bad things had happened since.

Sonny and Marta had a son, Thaddeus, eleven months after getting married, and seven weeks before the Robillards' daughter, Thekla, was born. They only had the one, while Irwin and Bunny gave birth to a second child a year later, a boy named Donovan. The day he was born, Sonny Blankenship bought controlling interest in Mountain Central Life Insurance Company based in Richmond. He immediately became CEO, a position he would hold until his death.

Mountain Central Life started selling insurance in all fifty states over the next several years. The venture steadily grew and began amassing cash. The operation moved to Lexington, where the Blankenships bought an ostentatious home along Richmond Road, near Idle Hour Country Club. They "held court" there and frequently had the Robillards join them for dinner. Thaddeus and Thekla struck up a romance while at the club, reaching a crescendo in marriage.

## FIFTY YEARS AGO

Irwin keyed open the red, hollow-metal door of the auction hall at 8:15 on a hot, hazy morning in August. Big gray arrows painted on the white walls of the building on both sides of the door had the words "ENTER HERE FOR AUCTIONS" stenciled on them in electric blue. A sinewy man of sixty, carrying something under his arm, eased out of a banged-up green Ford F150 truck. He wore khaki pants, a faded black T-shirt, and frayed red baseball cap. Irwin turned to greet the man. "What can I do for you, sir?"

"I wanted to know if you could auction off this antique for me." The man swiveled the wooden icon around and presented it for inspection. It was fourteen inches wide and twenty-one inches tall, and twice that width when folded open. The cover had a coat of arms painted on it, a gold shield dotted with seven big red balls, spanning front to back, split by the hinge-folded spine. On the inside, the left wing had a group of people looking up at a man on the right wing who was reclining atop a stack of ribbons that had Latin words inscribed on them.

"Is this the only thing you have?"

"Yes," the man replied with certainty.

Irwin pursed his lips and said, "Well, it's hard for us to sell one thing. There's a fee for the package of merchandise from each seller, and we take forty percent of the first thousand in proceeds on each item and twenty-five percent thereafter. We have to advertise, you know, and there are expenses associated with running an auction. How much you hoping to get for the piece?"

"If I could net a thousand dollars, I'd be happy," he said with a contrived smile.

"Look, why don't I just give you fifteen hundred for it now. Would save you a lot of hassle. I'll throw it in with another lot and hope to get my money back that way."

"Deal." The man stuck out his heavily tanned, knuckled hand to shake on it.

"Come on in. I'll write up a bill of sale and give you the cash." Later that day, Irwin dropped the item off at the office of the antique dealer he used for appraisals.

The dealer called back a week later, exhilaration in his voice. "Irwin, what you've got here is a tempura on oak diptych. They were almost always religious, portable worship accoutrements. This one is not. It may be extremely valuable."

Robillard, sitting at his walnut desk, leaned forward with interest and asked, "How so?"

"Well, the coat of arms is that of the Medici family of Florence, meaning that they may have commissioned the work. It's in the International Gothic style, which suggests it could be from the 1300s."

"Anything else?"

"Yes. The painter used a technique called *sgraffito*. That's where we get the word graffiti. You basically apply the paint over gold leaf and then partially scrape it away. There were very few artists around at that time who could pull off what's been done on this piece."

"So, who's the artist?"

"That's the interesting part. On the inside, the man on the right is Virgil, who escorted Dante through hell in *Dante's Inferno*, and on the left side are some of the characters they saw on their trip. The *Inferno* was released in 1314, and this work was probably done within twenty-five years by someone around Florence."

"Who?"

"Simone Martini. If I'm right, this diptych is worth millions."

Irwin leaned back in his chair, rubbed his forehead, and exhaled. "Have it checked out, but keep it confidential." He got up and walked out into the parking lot, lost in thought. Irwin took no notice of the road noise from I-75 beyond the ubiquitous rows of tobacco in the field to the west of where he stood. He wondered if he should tell Sonny about it.

## FIFTEEN YEARS AGO

Sonny Blankenship picked up the phone and dialed Irwin Robillard when he got to his office that morning. "Hey, how's it going?"

"Been slow. I think we've auctioned off everything that's for sale in Eastern Kentucky," Irwin remarked in his customary disconsolate manner.

Sonny, accustomed to his pessimism, offered, "This will cheer you up. Your son Donovan brought me a real estate development deal that I think Mountain Central is going to back. It's a mixed-use downtown high-rise. I'm getting his personal guarantee, and we'll share the profits. If the deal goes south, the company will take his interest in the property as additional collateral."

"Sonny, I can't auction off a distressed high-rise property for you. That's out of my league. You sure you want to do this?"

"I am. This town needs to become a regional center for bigger corporations. That way, we won't have to depend so much on farming, horse racing, and bourbon."

Irwin wanted to say something else, but decided to end the conversation. "You know best." For the next five years, the number of deals increased, many in big cities around the country, all backed by Mountain Central Life.

## TEN YEARS AGO

Irwin Robillard was standing at the auction house's freight dock when a call came in from Thaddeus Blankenship. "What's going on, Thad?"

"Dad dropped dead of a heart attack this morning sitting at his desk," he answered in a somber voice.

"What?"

"He was seventy-eight, Irwin. Well, you know that, you're the same age," Thaddeus allowed, on the verge of tears.

"I can't believe it. My condolences. He was a good man, the only friend I ever had. I'm sorry." Irwin felt a wave of sadness course through him.

"I'll be running Mountain Central now. I want you to know we'll be selling the auction business, and you'll have to retire. Dad set things up so you will receive a salary for the rest of your life. He always depended on you."

"Thanks for letting me know. How's your mother taking it?"

"Bad."

Marta Blankenship died thirteen months later of loneliness and despair.

Thaddeus, after assiduously studying Mountain's accounting information, was relieved to learn that the company was in good financial shape. That changed when the real estate market went into recession later in the year, and developers were taking "haircuts" and giving them to lenders backing their projects. Thaddeus knew loans were out on seven of his brother-in-law's projects, to the tune of $187 million. The first deal to fall apart was a project in Minneapolis. Mountain Life had to take possession of the property and auction it off for a net loss of $19 million. There were six more deals to get out of, and if the rest of them went like the first one, the life insurance business could come perilously close to not having enough cash reserves to pay claims. Thaddeus saw a way out.

Mountain Life entered the "high-risk" insurance market. Premiums were much larger and the risk greater, but in theory, if the right individuals were insured, big profits could be had on that business. Meanwhile, Donovan's real estate deals were slowly teetering on the brink. It took several years for all of them to wash out, and once they did, Thaddeus and Thekla were no longer on speaking terms with Donovan except through lawyers.

Writing risky insurance contracts kept Mountain Life alive until last year when, in desperate need of cash, the agents were told to relax the standards on business they accepted. The Kentucky Department of Insurance, after a serious look at the books, seized the company and declared it insolvent. The venture that Sonny Blankenship built into one of the nation's largest insurance firms was effectively bankrupt, and over 500 people found themselves without a job.

The Blankenship family was able to live off savings, but Donovan had to take a job selling men's clothing at a high-end haberdashery. Because he was well known, Donovan sold a lot of suits and ties. He was at retirement age and would be living on social security and his salesman's wages. He had nothing else, at least at the moment.

## THIS MORNING

Donovan stepped through the door and shouted, "Dad, you here?" He was lugging the Martini diptych under his arm. The fetid air in the house smelled like stale urine. He heard his father getting up from the table in the kitchen. "I've brought your Martini back."

Irwin walked into view and replied, "Thank you." He smiled and asked, "Would you do me a favor? Here is the key to a small climate-controlled locker that I rent over on Tates Creek Road. The address of the place is on the keyring. Can you take it over there? I don't want it in the house anymore." He handed the key to his son.

"Sure, Dad. I'll run it over and bring the key right back. I've got to get to work." He stopped at the door and turned to face his father. "One of these days, we need to talk about getting you some help in here to do the cleaning and wash, or maybe you should consider moving into an assisted living facility."

Irwin looked away, saying, "Your sister brings me breakfast and coffee every morning. I like that arrangement. No use changing it."

"She won't talk to me anymore, so would you ask her to help you with the wash? It doesn't smell very good in here." Donovan pulled the door shut behind him before his father could emote.

Thekla entered her father's house the following Thursday morning and got no response when she called his name. He always sat at the kitchen table, waiting for her to arrive. His face would light up when she came in. She reminded him of Bunny. Those were the only pleasant thoughts he had left in his diminished, haphazard life. Thekla found her father face down in his bed. He was dead.

## FOUR MONTHS LATER

Irwin Robillard's two children and son-in-law sat around the heavily oiled cherry table in the attorney's conference room, ready to hear Irwin's will. He started off by saying, "Strangely enough, Mister Robillard revised this will just a few days before he died. Everything is in order, and it's legal because we did the work."

Thekla remarked, "My father always trusted your firm."

The attorney went on, "So, this is about as simple as a will can get. Mister Robillard had three classes of assets and no debt. Two of the assets were cash and the house he lived in. They go to Donovan. The third was his non-cash personal property. That would be everything in the house that isn't nailed down plus a piece of art stored in a rented locker. Those things go to Thekla. Here is the key to the locker."

"Is that the old, folded painting on wood that was around the house forever?" Thekla asked. She began to feel like she had just gotten the shaft.

"I wouldn't know, ma'am. There is one more thing here. It's a letter addressed to Thaddeus." He slid the envelope across the table. Thaddeus opened it and read the note inside three times.

*Thaddeus,*

*I bought the artwork your wife is inheriting fifty years ago for $1,500 from a guy that came into the auction hall one day. I had the piece authenticated. It was painted by Simone Martini in the 1300s, and is worth at least $3,000,000. I should have told your father about it and would have had I sold it. Maybe this will make up for some of the losses your family sustained in the insurance business. Thekla should have the key for the locker. Take Donovan with you. He knows where the unit is located. There is something there for him too.*

*Irwin Robillard*

Donovan asked, "What does the letter say?" Thaddeus threw it back across the table to him.

When the three of them walked into the air-conditioned hallway in front of the orange storage lockers for rent, Donovan stepped forward and shot a finger at a unit on the end. "I think this is the one. Dad had me put the painting in here a few days before he died."

Thaddeus tried the key. It didn't work. He read the number on the keyring as he scanned down the row. When he saw the right unit, he said, "This is it." He opened the door to find the Martini diptych and a small package, which had a letter to Thekla and a key for another locker in it.

*Thekla,*

*I made the mistake years ago of telling Donovan how valuable the Martini was. I expected him to steal it and try to sell it when he got into financial trouble, which he did.*

*That's why I had a replica made of the piece. I'm sure he made a replica of the fake he stole from me, thinking that it was the real thing. He brought his fake back to me, and I had him put it in a locker up the row from here. The key to that unit is with this letter. I think you know how to handle it from here.*

*Your Loving Father*

Thekla held the letter and other key in her left hand as she carefully relocked the authentic Martini diptych with her right. She said, "Let's get out of here."

"Wait, I thought there was something for me," Donovan whined.

"I'll tell you when we get outside." In the parking lot, near their cars, she said, "Thad, get in." He got behind the wheel and slammed the door. Thekla looked at her brother in total disgust and announced, "Dad left you a Martini too." She threw the key at him. It bounced off his stomach.

"That son of a bitch," Donovan growled as he bent down.

On the way home, Thaddeus contemplated when the right time would be to tell his wife that he had smothered her father to death with a pillow the night she was out late with her girlfriends. After all, Irwin's rotten son had ruined the Blankenship family, and having to pay Irwin's salary in retirement was tiresome. He did feel a tick of remorse, however, when he thought about the diptych. Nonetheless, he would wait to tell Thekla until after he killed her brother.

# BEE HARMED AND DANGEROUS

In the Cracker Barrel parking lot, just off the I-75 exit near Berea, the sporadic summer wind blew the whining sounds of decelerating engines through in waves as big rigs and coal trucks coasted intermittently down the first of many long hills to come on the busy Eastern Kentucky highway.

Inside, a husky man named Peter Moran sat at a rustic table, scanning the menu with disinterest. He had on a burnt-orange golf shirt with the words *Owsley Honey* stitched on the left sleeve, which did little to divert attention away from his unusually short arms and calloused hands. He stood up suddenly when Marvin Canfield came into the dining hall and began walking toward him. Peter stuck out his hand to shake and asked, "How's it going?" before sitting down again.

"Bad."

"How so?"

Marvin looked vacantly at the wall and flipped his right hand in disgust. He wore black denim bib overalls and a tan short-sleeved shirt. Like his father and two brothers, Marvin was a tall, slender man with a dark complexion, Andy Griffith hair, and a set of dazzling white teeth that were all his. "Somebody stole my inventory of Ray Harm prints." He dropped into the chair across from Peter and leaned forward to glare at his brother-in-law.

The Morans and Canfields feuded from the Civil War to World War I. It started when one family sided with the south and the other the north. The bad blood ended after more than a hundred deaths when a teenager from each family went to die in "The Great War."

"Who would do such a thing? How much were they worth?" Peter probed.

"Fifty thousand or so." The limited-edition prints were counterfeit and hadn't cost him that much, but it was the principle of the thing.

"Look, if you need any money, I'll float you." Peter searched for an answer in Marvin's body language.

"No, I'll find them. So, what's on your mind?"

Moran shifted in his seat and drew a folded paper out of the back pocket of his trousers. "I found this nailed to a stud inside the wall when I was remodeling the house. I'm not sure what to make of it." He unfolded the note and handed it over.

Marvin read it several times before a sullen expression overtook his face. "Well, how long after this did it happen?" He pushed the note back in Peter's direction.

"Six weeks." The waitress appeared at the end of the table to take their order. "We'll have the fried chicken, mashed potatoes and gravy, green beans, and corn bread," Peter said politely.

~ ~ ~

Bees make honey for one reason, to have something to eat during the winter. The female worker bees starve the drones as cold weather sets in because of the notion that there may not be enough food to go around. After all, a drone did nothing more than roll in the hay with "queenie" when the weather was good, which explained why he ended up paying the ultimate price. Nature hath no fury like a female worker bee scorned.

A healthy colony produces fifty pounds of honey a year. Forty pounds of it can be taken without cutting into what the bees need to live on during hibernation. Luckily, when the warm sun shines, bees make honey. Lots of it. Peter Moran learned how to capitalize on that propitious occurrence. He sprinkled hives all over the property that his wife Holly owned in Owsley County, Kentucky, on the western edge of the eastern coalfield.

Holly Moran and Winona Canfield were the only children of the deceased Martha and Jeff White of Booneville, the county seat of Owsley. Martha died giving birth to Winona, and Jeff worked at a truck-axle factory in Berea to put food on the table, until he was found dead sitting in front of the television at the new house that he had just finished building. Soon after his death, Holly married Peter Moran, and Winona got hitched to Marvin Canfield.

When his girls were seventeen and eighteen, White was approached by an energy company that offered to harvest coal on his property by employing what they aptly called "mountain-top removal." His tract of land was alongside Upper Burning Creek, named for the natural spring known to bubble up with crude oil from time to time that would catch fire. It quit doing that when the "holler fill" covered over the spring with the top of the mountain lopped off to get at the coal seam.

White made the mining company put back three feet of topsoil instead of the customary one foot. He insisted on rich alluvial loam that would support the natural flower gardens he intended to plant among the dozens of varieties of trees he planned to put in. Acres and acres of pansies, mint, liatris, snowdrops, lavender, bee balm, goldenrod, sage, pussy willow, zinnias, marigolds, and phlox were sown wild over the quaint plateau left behind after the coal had been savagely removed. The front corner of the land was kept barren for a house to be built with the rest of the money Jeff White received from the mining company.

The modern abode had a flat roof, two bedrooms and a Jack-and-Jill bathroom upstairs for his teenage girls, master bedroom and bath on the main floor, and floor-to-ceiling glass windows in parts of the kitchen and family room. The poured-in-place concrete floor was set in a grid of herringbone wood strips. The limestone fireplace, with its chimney rising above the second floor, sat in the center of the main floor, open on both sides. Wood siding on the exterior was painted a glossy-white enamel, and the fascia and trim were made of black metal.

White's last will and testament gave the house to Winona and acreage to Holly. The fields were adorned with pollen-rich flowers. Holly didn't much like the outdoors, so she talked Peter into hiring her sister Winona to help with the bees. He added new colonies each year and eked out a living selling the honey crop to grocery chains until something very unexpected happened.

Two years ago, a group of doctors conducted tests on honeys to see what medicinal properties could be found. Manuka honey from New Zealand, costing a duke's ransom, was touted in Asia as a general cure-all. The other brands tested were to be measured against it. Owsley Honey turned out to have a rich variety of beneficial chemical compounds, including the same amount of MGO and DHA found in manuka honey.

One of the doctors conducting the study flew to Kentucky forthwith, drove to Booneville, and put a million-dollar check in Peter Moran's hand to buy 80 percent of his honey production for the next year, no matter the amount of the harvest. The only conditions were that the transaction and name of the buyer be kept confidential. Peter didn't speak a word of the deal to Holly or Winona.

Holly did notice, when she signed the joint tax return in the spring, their income and taxes had skyrocketed. She kept that to herself and chose not to question Peter about it.

Last summer, the colorful fields visible in all directions were laden with a host of flowers and pollen. The view over the mountains of Kentucky and the pleasant smell of the plethora of blooms were intoxicating. When hive #38 needed to be stripped of honey, Peter carefully pulled up a full comb and handed it to Winona. She turned to him and spoke loudly through her beekeeper's suit, "I think she knows."

He hesitated and then added, "She's insanely jealous, and if she knew for sure, I think she'd divorce me. That would be bad since this property is in her name."

"So, what are we going to do?"

"Would you consider selling me your house?" He carefully dislodged a second comb from the hive. "What if I paid you cash for it and also deeded over the house that Holly and I live in to you and Marvin. I think he'd go for that because he knows he has no stake in your house since it's in your name." Winona looked up, deep in thought. "That way, he'll end up getting some equity on a swap if our house is put in both of your names."

Winona had frizzy auburn hair, earth hands, and a natural beauty that men, including Peter, found captivating. Her round, freckled face formed a smile as she inquired, "How much are you willing to pay?"

"Name the price."

~ ~ ~

Marvin Canfield had never worked an honest day in his life. Winona fell for him because he was handsome and well spoken. He'd been gambling on the ponies since the age of fifteen and was still doing it four days a week. He met a guy at the OTB right out of high school who offered to sell him an annual allotment of counterfeit Ray Harm prints at fifteen dollars apiece. Marvin forged Harm's signature on each lot he bought and went around selling the copies to art stores and gift shops at $250 a pop. He averaged eight to ten sales a week, tax free of course, unless or until he got caught.

Canfield always bet the same way, a five-dollar exacta part-wheel on the three horses with the lowest odds on top, and two horses with the lowest odds on the bottom, which amounted to four bets costing twenty dollars a race. Using low-odds horses meant that a winning ticket would never be big enough to draw the attention of the IRS. He would bet a total of $500 on the first twenty-five races that were run in a day. He usually cashed seven or eight tickets and broke even. He often won more than eight races, and rarely hit on less than seven.

Peter and Holly began remodeling the original White house that they bought from Winona late last year. It took them six months to gut, refit, and update the place into something worth living in. A chamber for accepting bee deliveries was added to the back of the building, which had a door to the outside and one off an interior hall that could be locked from the inside for security purposes. The final step was to redo the walls in the kitchen and family room. That's where Moran found the note.

Peter's cell phone rang as he was returning to Owsley County after the delicious fried-chicken lunch he'd just had at Cracker Barrel. The caller's number came up as Marvin's. "Pete, we've got to get to the bottom of this thing. Why don't you and Holly invite us over for dinner this Friday night so we can try to get some answers?"

"I'll have Holly coordinate it with Winona. Are you worried about something?"

Marvin capped the conversation off. "Yeah. Have that note handy."

Holly Moran was an attractive woman in a sophisticated way. Her eyes were hazel, hair straight brown, and on Friday night, she was wearing a sleeveless white blouse, chartreuse skirt, and brown pumps. Holly knew how to throw a good dinner party. She hadn't put on a spread like this since she and her sister lived there when the place was first built.

Peter greeted Winona and Marvin as they came through the door. The two couples went into the family room, where a drink cart with a dozen bourbons was set up next to the wall. The appetizers of expensive cheeses, crackers, and salami were laid out artfully on the coffee table. Marvin said, "Boy, you guys did a great job re-modeling the place. Thanks for inviting us over." The background music by Erroll Garner echoed through the room in loud and quiet stretches while the foursome made pleasant conversation.

Marvin pulled Peter aside when the girls were talking and quietly asked him to hand over the note.

Holly stood up with a start and said, "Oh Peter, I forgot to tell you that a crate of bees was delivered this afternoon. You might want to check on them."

Winona walked over to Peter and said, "I'll go with you." The two of them headed down the hall toward the back of the house. When they got there, the large crate loaded with bees could be seen through the small piece of glass in the hollow metal door to the chamber room. They stepped inside and heard the door latch behind them. As Peter picked the crate up to inspect it, the front side fell open toward him. In an instant, Winona and Peter were covered with frenzied brown carpets of bees. They frantically swatted them off only to increase the number of stings. Winona tried the door to the outside to no avail, and Peter pounded on the locked one leading into the house. Holly and Marvin heard nothing over Garner's elaborate introduction to "Misty." Winona and Peter were lying face down in the chamber room, stung to death, when Marvin found them.

News broke of the grisly deaths the next morning. By late in the day, the doctor who had the contract for 80 percent of the honey production called Holly to introduce himself and express condolences. He mentioned that when things settled down, he wanted to make an offer to run the bee farm with his crew. He would pay her a handsome royalty for every pound of Owsley Honey he took out. A deal was in place two months later that paid Holly a substantial fee for doing absolutely nothing.

Owsley County, Kentucky, had the distinction of being the poorest white county in the United States. Holly's earnings were bending the median income upward among the four thousand or so county residents, but Marvin Canfield was still doing his part to hold it down. All he had to his name were the house he lived in and a few dollars in his pocket. Canfield still hadn't recovered the Ray Harm prints that had been stolen from him.

Holly Moran opened the front door of her house on an early Saturday evening to see Marvin standing there with a nasty grin on his face. "Can I come in, Holly?" The day's light was all but gone.

"Sure." She stepped aside and ushered him into the family room. "Can I get you something to drink?"

"No, thanks." He sat down on the chair across from the sofa where she had seated herself, arms crossed.

"So, I take it you didn't come by for a lavish dinner. What can I do for you?"

"Oh, I was just wondering if there was a chance we might strike up a romance." Marvin widened his eyes and stuck out his chin.

Holly guffawed, leaned back on the sofa cushion, and threw her arms toward the ceiling. "You're kidding, right? You don't have two nickels to rub together, not to mention the fact that you were married to my sister."

"You're forgetting one thing: I can rat you out for rigging the bee box and locks on the chamber-room doors. That could get you sent up for killing your husband and sister. You certainly had good reason to. We both knew they were lovebirds."

Holly stood and walked over to the floor-length window that looked down the mountain. A few dim lights were twinkling on the ridge of the hill across the way. No cars were moving on the winding road leading out of the hollow. "I figured you'd pull a stunt like this." She turned back around and displayed her own version of a nasty grin. "I kept a key to our old house. I'm the one that lifted your stack of phony Harms. Winona told me all about your print scam, you know."

Marvin laughed in her face. "I can get more where those came from."

She fired back, "I took them to my attorney and told him to rat you out if anything bad happened to me."

"Touché! So, everything should work out fine between us once you put me on the payroll." Marvin stood up and took his turn in front of the window.

"Not a chance." Holly sat again and reached for her phone that was on the edge of the coffee table.

"You'll reconsider when you see this. It's a photocopy of the original." She got up and walked over to where he was standing to take the sheet of paper out of his hand.

*June 7, 1998*

*I overheard my daughter Holly talking to her sister while I was building this house. She was saying that she blamed me for not taking her mother to the hospital quickly enough right after Winona's birth to save her from bleeding to death. Holly was one at the time and couldn't have known what really happened. I know how she can be. If I'm found dead soon after the date on this note, you can be sure that Holly or Winona killed me.*

*Jeff White*

Marvin said, "You know, you married a Moran, and that makes you one of them. Us Canfields don't like Morans."

"What's that got to do with anything?" Holly backed away from him and stood behind the sofa.

"Winona married me. She became a Canfield. You, as a Moran, ended up with everything and never lifted a finger. You talked Winona into doing all the hard work with the bees and probably talked her into killing your father." Suddenly, he drew a pepper-box pistol that had been tucked behind his pants belt and shot her in the torso six times. She fell backward and dropped her phone.

Not more than two seconds after that, the floor-to-ceiling glass window that Marvin stood in front of exploded, and the rat-a-tat-tat of a semi-automatic rifle could be heard before he fell face forward on the carpet. The shooter worked his way down the hill and got in a black Porsche parked on the side of the road and sped off.

Holly, near death, reached for her phone and called 911. She only had the strength to utter, "Marvin Canfield shot me." The police were not yet aware that Canfield lay dead next to her, so they put out an APB, considering him to be armed and dangerous.

~ ~ ~

The doctor with the honey contract came into court several weeks later and presented an option he had gotten from Holly Moran to buy the house and bee-farm property. The judge asked him to state his name. "Doctor Derek Moran, sir. Holly's husband and I were cousins."

The judge leaned back in his chair and said, "I'd watch my back if I were you. The Canfield and Moran feud is back on. The first one lasted seventy-five years."

Little did he know that the doctor had already killed his first Canfield.

www.ingramcontent.com/pod-product-compliance
Lightning Source LLC
Chambersburg PA
CBHW011116100726
47898CB00011B/3117